"It Looks Like We're Going To Be Neighbors,"

Alison said haltingly, her face suffused with color.

Rafe drew a sharp breath, and she was aware of him stiffening. "How do you figure that?"

Lifting her chin slightly, she said, "It's obvious you're setting up shop, and since I am, too, I thought—"

"You thought what?" Rafe cut in.

Although her flush deepened, Alison refused to be put off by his abrupt manner. "I thought I'd introduce myself," she finished lamely.

"I see."

But he didn't. The mocking glint in his eye along with his tone clearly said, Lady, what the hell are you doing here?

Which was a good question. What *was* she doing here, standing uncomfortably in front of him, trembling like some teenager on her first date? Alison felt as if she were on fire....

Dear Reader:

Happy New Year! Now that the holiday rush is through you can sit down, kick off your shoes and open the cover of a Silhouette Desire.

As you might know, we'll be continuing the *Man of the Month* program through 1990. In the upcoming year look for men created by some of your favorite authors: Elizabeth Lowell, Annette Broadrick, Diana Palmer, Nancy Martin and Ann Major. Also, we'll be presenting Barbara Boswell's first-Desire-ever as a *Man of the Month*.

But Desire is more than the *Man of the Month*. Each and every book is a wonderful love story in which the emotional and the sensual go hand-in-hand. The book can be humorous or serious, but it will always be satisfying.

So whether you're a first-time reader or a regular, welcome to Desire 1990—I know you're going to be pleased.

Lucia Macro
Senior Editor

MARY LYNN BAXTER

WINTER HEAT

SILHOUETTE *Desire*

Published by Silhouette Books New York

America's Publisher of Contemporary Romance

SILHOUETTE BOOKS
300 East 42nd St., New York, N.Y. 10017

ISBN: 0-373-05542-0

First Silhouette Books printing January 1990

Printed in the U.S.A.

MARY LYNN BAXTER

sold hundreds of romances before she ever wrote one. The D & B Bookstore, right on the main drag in Lufkin, Texas, is her home as well as the store she owns and manages. She and her husband, Leonard, garden in their spare time. Around five o'clock every evening they can be found picking butter beans on their small farm just outside of town.

Monroe, Texas needed an addition, a lift to its existing retail stores, and Alison had determined that Silk Reflections was going to be it. The compulsion to do something constructive with her time had begun building inside her shortly after she'd found her husband, Carter, lying dead on the floor. He had suffered a massive heart attack.

Once the numbing shock had worn off, loneliness had become her number one enemy. The awesome affliction was something to loathe and fear, to resist and dread. Today, two years later, she was still battling that intrusive force that would destroy her as surely as heart failure had destroyed her husband. Loneliness was poisoning her.

Still it was more than the loneliness that drove her now. It was the craving to be useful, to be needed once again.

She knew that part of her problem stemmed from the fact that her sister, Heather, was away at college and no longer needed her. But then Heather, aged twenty, hadn't needed her in a long time. Still, it wasn't easy to admit that her sister was now a grown woman.

Alison had been married to Carter when her parents were killed in an automobile accident. Heather, who had been only nine years old at the time, had come to live with them, and became more like a daughter than a sister.

If only she and Carter... No, she refused to think about the child they hadn't had. Besides, she had stopped fretting about that long ago.

One

She saw him again. He was doing the same thing to-day that he'd been doing yesterday—unloading planks of wood from the back of a pickup truck.

As if thoroughly captivated by something so insignificant, so mundane, Alison Young continued to stand transfixed in front of the window and watch the stranger. But in reality her mind was miles away.

Finally, with a mental shake, she turned around and once again surveyed the empty room.

"I can do it," she muttered aloud, walking toward the wall in front of her, envisioning with every step she took shelves littered with silk flower arrangements in all sizes, shapes and prices. "I know I can make it work."

Vexed, Alison ran an unsteady hand over her silvery blond hair. She had wound it into a chic, tight chignon at the nape of her neck. If only her anxiety could be controlled as easily as her hair.

She shook her head, impatient with her own self-pity. Feeling sorry for herself was not the answer. She wasn't the only woman to unexpectedly and tragically lose her husband.

Even though she was a widow, Alison had much to be thankful for. She had Heather, and she had more money than she could ever spend, a lovely home, friends, her health—and at age thirty-five she still had a better than average face and figure. Even as she thought this, she caught a glimpse of herself in the mirror on the back of the door and gazed with objective appraisal at her own reflection.

A delicate face with small, precise features stared back at her. Her husband had often told her she resembled a young Grace Kelly. And while she was blessed with full breasts and a small waist, it was her eyes that commanded the most attention. They were an unusual smoky lavender.

In addition to her physical attributes, she was intelligent and capable and hoped to do something more than attend endless parties and play endless rounds of bridge.

When Carter was alive, their limited activities were enough because that was what he'd wanted her to do. But no longer. She needed a challenge. Switching from socialite to businesswoman would suffice.

Jockeying her time between her flower shop and her volunteer work at the Women's Shelter of East Texas would fill her days. Then at night she would be so tired she'd fall instantly to sleep without thinking about how cold and empty her bed was.

Suddenly a chill descended over her as reality reared its ugly head. Was she deluding herself? While anticipation and excitement coursed through her, so did fear—fear of failure, fear of her friends saying, "We hate to say it, but we told you so."

Despite her misgivings, Alison was finally going to share her plan with three of her closest friends, and in doing so hopefully garner their best wishes.

Knowing she had a few more minutes to wait before they arrived, she wandered aimlessly back to the window and looked out. The man next door was still there. He had worked his way closer to the property division line, which enabled her to get a better view of him. She wasn't sure what he was doing because she was suddenly too busy admiring the way the muscles bunched in a massive set of bare shoulders each time he lifted the hammer above his head.

Perspiration gleamed like early morning dew on the bare sunkissed skin, and for a moment she was held spellbound.

"Not bad," she murmured. Then realizing what she was doing, she shook her head savagely, while a dull flush rose in her cheeks. It was out of character for her to eye a man, any man, so blatantly.

Still, she didn't turn away. Squinting, Alison leaned closer to the windowpane; this time she saw that he was building some type of stands.

Even though it was November, he seemed oblivious to the chill in the air as he busily cut and nailed long strips of wood together. His face was in plain view, and she saw that it bore the stamp of exhaustion. Moreover, he seemed alone and unhappy, a feeling she could identify with. But mentally, she saluted him, certain that hard work was the panacea for those ailments.

Suddenly, as if he sensed he was being watched, the man stopped hammering and looked up. And stared. Alison, conscious of an unexpected quickness of her pulse, boldly returned his stare.

It was only after he moved, contorting his lips in a cynical smile, that Alison relaxed. Confused, she quickly averted her gaze, but not before every detail about the stranger was embedded in her brain: the almost black hair, the face with strong, irregularly balanced features, the tall, rangy frame with worn jeans riding dangerously low on the hips.

Overall he had a rumpled look, as though he could easily have just crawled out of bed and dressed on the run. And the rugged, haphazard image did nothing to detract from his hard-edged good looks.

"You're losing it, Alison Young," she muttered. Yet she couldn't stop herself from stealing another glance, and attempted to assure her interest was merely curiosity.

She swallowed hard, and to her dismay felt a tremor of excitement dart through her. Minutes later her heart was still pumping hard and confusion still warred within her when she hurried to the door in answer to the loud knock.

"Well, it's about time," an auburn-haired, freckle-faced woman exclaimed as she breezed across the threshold.

The woman's name was June Reeves, and she was Alison's best friend. Her only fault, Alison thought with a smile, was her mouth; she talked incessantly. There were times when Alison longed to stuff a sock in it to shut her up. Nevertheless, she was a doll, and Alison loved her dearly.

"And hello to you, too," Alison said good-naturedly, stepping aside and holding the door open while two other women filed past.

The tall, regal one was Myra Kelly. The other, short and plump with premature gray hair, was Natalie Kent. All were married to three of the town's leading citizens.

The man next door totally forgotten, Alison smiled at her friends who were now standing in the center of the room with puzzled expressions on their faces.

"Okay, Alison," Myra said, her strong features pinched into a frown, "what have you got up your sleeve? It's obvious you didn't invite us to your rent house to play bridge."

"Yeah, honey," Natalie chimed in, "what's going on?"

"You sure you're all right?" Although June's tone was less abrasive, it, too, held skepticism.

Alison's smile broadened into a full-fledged grin. "I've never been better, ladies."

June's eyes lighted to match her red hair. "Ah-ha, you've met a man."

"Not hardly," Alison replied lightly.

June's face fell. "Okay, so what's behind the smug look you're wearing like a gaudy neon sign?"

"I've decided to go to work, that's what." There, she had said it. Now all she had to do was wait for the fireworks.

"Work!" Their shrieks were almost in unison.

"Yes, work," Alison mimicked, her grin still intact. "I'm going to turn this vacant rent house into a silk flower shop and operate it myself."

"Oh, honey, no," June wailed. "You can't mean that?"

Alison didn't so much as blink. "Of course I mean it, June. And you, of all people, should know that. This is something I've been wanting to do for a long time, and now that Heather's in college..."

"But...but why...?" June began, only to be interrupted by Myra.

"If you ask me, she's taken leave of her senses."

"No, Myra, I haven't taken leave of my senses," Alison explained patiently, refusing to let Myra's attitude rile her. "Just the opposite, in fact. I've finally gotten control of them."

Natalie gave an uncharacteristic snort and waved a plump hand. "I beg to differ with you, dear friend. I know that Carter's death was a shock and extremely hard on you, but to contemplate going to work—that's absurd."

"For heaven's sake, Natalie," Alison snapped, exasperated, "you sound as if work is synonymous with AIDS, that it's something terrible, something to be shunned."

The women looked at one another and shrugged.

"That's exactly how we feel," Myra said, opting to speak for the others. "Why, just the thought of working leaves a bad taste in my mouth." As if to qualify her feelings, she shuddered visibly.

"Seriously, Alison," June said softly, her expression troubled, "why do you want to go to work?" She paused. "Surely it's not money."

Alison sighed again, giving in to her growing frustration. "No, June, it's not money. I couldn't possibly spend all the money Carter left me."

"Then why?" Natalie asked, and shifted her more than ample body closer to Myra, as if she needed an ally. "If you do go through with this scheme of yours, what will we do for a fourth at our bridge games?" she added on a petulant wail.

"That's exactly why I'm going to work," Alison said flatly, her gaze encompassing them all. "I'm fed up with the social scene. I can't imagine spending the rest of my life just playing bridge or swinging a tennis racket."

"You didn't feel that way when Carter was alive," Myra responded snidely.

Alison's lips thinned. "No, you're right, I didn't. But when he died, my life changed."

"I know it did, honey," June rushed to say with sympathy, giving Myra a hard look. "But going into business is a big responsibility as well as a risk," she added, then turned back to face Alison, her small face screwed into lines of thought. "Not to mention tying you down."

"But even so, I'm looking forward to the responsibility, the challenge. What with Heather off at school, I feel—"

"Speaking of Heather," Natalie interrupted, "have you told her?"

Alison hesitated. "No, as a matter of fact I haven't. But I intend to rectify that the first time she comes home."

Myra said, "Well, I can tell you right now, she's not going to like it."

"What about Arthur?" June asked. "What does he say?"

"Now that's the answer to your boredom," Myra broke in, her eyes sparking. "Arthur. Why not marry him? Lord knows, he's been after you ever since Carter died."

Instantly an image of Arthur Hamilton, widower and successful businessman, popped into Alison's mind. Medium height, medium build, medium everything. But very sweet, very understanding and very predictable.

"Arthur's a friend, nothing more, and you all know that." When Natalie would have interrupted, Alison held up her hand and went on, "Anyway, believe it or not, I'm finally reaching a point where being part of a matched set is no longer important."

"Okay, then," Myra said, seemingly unaffected by the sudden chill in Alison's tone, "think of what people will say. I can just hear them now. 'How awful, Alison going to work!' Can't you?"

"I could care less about what they say," Alison replied, her tone even.

Although Alison considered all three women close friends, she thought the least of Myra. Her snobbery was more than a mere affectation.

Myra raised a perfectly arched brow. "That's what you say now, but what about later?"

"It still won't make a difference," Alison said calmly, though on the inside she was far from calm. She was seething. Their digs and shortsightedness hurt, but she refused to let it show because it really didn't matter what they said or thought. She was committed to her plan, even if she encountered the same prejudices from her sister. "I'm through letting others dictate my life."

Following a moment of awkward silence, the women began chatting at leisure, as if they sensed they had gone far enough in their criticism. Deliberately tuning out their conversation, Alison turned her back and made her way across the room to a desk and chair, the only furniture in the room. She was about to sit when Myra's strident voice halted her.

"What did you say, Myra?" Alison asked, straightening to full height.

Smacking her lips, Myra continued staring out the window. "I said, what a hunk."

Without looking, Alison knew to whom she was referring.

"Who's a hunk?" Natalie asked, hurrying to stand beside Myra. After gawking herself, she suddenly whipped back around, grinned and motioned for June. "Move it, honey, you've gotta see this."

"Tut-tut, Alison," Myra gushed. "You've been holding out on us. No wonder you like to spend time here."

Though Alison was glad she was no longer the center of conversation, for some crazy and unexplainable reason she resented them turning their attention to the man next door.

"Do you know who he is?" June asked, still staring out the window alongside the others.

"No," Alison answered reluctantly.

"Well, I do."

All eyes focused on Myra.

She tossed back her mane of black hair as if on stage, then added, "If I'm not mistaken, and I know I'm not, he's Rafe Beaumont. And he's only recently come back to town."

"Who?" Natalie asked, frowning.

"Oh, you know...." Myra slapped the air with a hand. "The Beaumonts who started growing Christmas trees on their farm some time back. There was an article in the paper. Well, the old man's dead now, and the prodigal son's apparently come back to cut and sell the trees."

"So that's what he's doing," Alison remarked more to herself than to them.

June looked at Natalie and winked. "Well, I for one know where I'm going to get my Christmas tree."

"I'm surprised you know so much about them," Alison said sarcastically, "especially since they don't move in your social circles."

Alison's sarcasm didn't seem to faze Myra in the least. "Gossip, my dear, gossip," she said airily.

Alison was becoming more puzzled by the second. "But why on earth would anyone be gossiping about Rafe Beaumont?"

"Ah, I've got your attention now, don't I?" Myra grinned slyly.

"Come on, Myra," June said, "cut the theatrics and tell us."

"All right," Myra said, lowering her voice to a hushed, conspiratorial whisper. "The reason people are talking is because that gorgeous hunk has served time in the penitentiary at Huntsville. My dears, he's an ex-con."

Two

─────

An *Ex-con!* Alison was stunned, though why she hadn't the foggiest idea, except that for some crazy reason Rafe Beaumont had struck a strange chord within her. She had identified with him, and the thought of him having served time was abhorrent.

She wasn't the only one who was shocked. Natalie's hyper voice forced Alison out of her thoughts. "You mean that good-looking specimen's been in the pen?"

"That's right," Myra announced. And almost proudly, too, as though she had performed her duty to God and country by delivering that juicy tidbit.

Alison shook her head as if to clear it, suddenly disgusted with the turn the conversation had taken.

Yet she couldn't refrain from looking hard at Myra and asking, "Are you sure?"

"I'm sure," Myra declared, her gaze still pinned on Rafe Beaumont. "If you put any stock in gossip, that is. And I've found that where there's smoke there's fire."

Unfortunately what Myra said was true, Alison reminded herself, especially in a small town.

"Oh, come on Alison," Myra went on, "surely you've heard of the Beaumonts. Why the old man was known all over town for his drunken escapades."

Alison hadn't heard. Although she had lived in Monroe for years, she hadn't been born and reared there. She had grown up in Dallas. Because she and Carter had moved in the upper echelon, there were many townspeople she did not know.

"Mmm, nice tush," June was saying with a grin.

"And shoulders," Natalie inserted.

All three were at the window, their necks extended.

"For crying out loud," Alison said, her tone more than mildly annoyed, "you're all acting like you've never seen a good-looking man before."

June spun around and grinned at Alison, then winked. "Aw come on, honey, stop acting like some ole fuddy-duddy. Anyway, it's all right to look as long as you don't touch, right?"

In spite of herself, Alison smiled. "You have a point, I guess. Still, what if he sees you ogling him like he's on display in a circus?" Suddenly she felt her face turn beet red. How could she condemn them for doing the same thing she'd been doing only moments before their arrival? And she had gotten caught.

"So what?" Myra gushed in response to Alison's question. "Anyone with a gut like he's got deserves to be stared at. Just look at it!"

"I'm looking, I'm looking," Natalie said, her more than ample bosom heaving in her chest.

"Mmm, I wonder how he'd be in the sack?" Myra mused.

June, standing next to Myra, poked her in the ribs and grinned. "Hey, watch it, woman. If Robert knew you were talking like that about another man, he'd cut off your allowance."

"He could try, you mean," Myra shot back with a confident ring in her voice. "Only I'd cut him off." She faced June with eyebrows raised. "And you know what *I* mean."

Natalie snickered and turned toward Alison, who was still at her desk, riffling through the papers on it, trying her best to ignore the relentless prattle. "Hey, trot your bones over here and join us."

"No, thank you," Alison responded. Then seeing Natalie's round face crumple, she tempered her sharp tone and smiled. "I've already seen him. I know how easy on the eye he is."

"You got that right," June wheezed, comically fanning herself. "Praise the Lord you noticed. My faith in you is restored."

Alison rolled her eyes. "Come on, friend. Give me a break."

June laughed. "Not on your life, not until you drop that icy reserve and show an interest in the opposite sex again."

"And you think Rafe Beaumont is the place to start?"

Alison's softly spoken question brought on a silence that would rival an audience at an execution. Three pairs of indignant eyes swung in her direction.

June was the first to break the silence, her face flushed. "Of course not, silly. You're deliberately being obtuse."

Myra harrumphed and ran a hand through her silver-tipped black hair. "Beautiful as he may be, darling," she drawled, "I hardly think someone who's served time for stealing cars and selling them is someone you should get involved with."

June's hand flew to her throat. "Is that what he did, steal cars?"

"Yep," Myra responded, her gaze on Alison.

"Why would he do something like that?" Natalie asked, round-eyed.

Myra spoke again. "Maybe because he was dirt poor. Who knows? But Rafe Beaumont was always a bad boy, a very bad boy."

"Maybe he's changed," Alison pointed out, shocking herself. Why had she felt the need to defend a complete stranger? She had no idea whether Rafe Beaumont had changed or not, and furthermore she couldn't care less. Maybe it was Myra's "holier-than-thou" attitude that prodded her into speaking so rashly. Sometimes it got on her nerves, and now was one of those times.

"Oh, grow up, Alison." Myra's tone was as sharp as it was condescending. "Men like Rafe Beaumont never change. Once bad, always bad."

"Not necessarily," Alison said testily. "Apparently his run-in with the law happened when he was much younger. For all you know, he could turn out to be a model citizen. Maybe he already is."

Natalie's lips thinned. "I doubt that."

"Well, for the sake of throwing a damper on this party," Alison said, "who cares?"

"I couldn't agree with you more, Natalie," Myra spoke up, as if Alison hadn't said a word. She moved slightly to lean against the window facing. "However, word has it that he's doing carpentry work and is damn good at it."

Something clicked inside Alison's mind, and she lifted her head. "Did you say carpenter?"

"Sure did. Why?"

June swung around, her eyes wide. "Alison Young, you're not thinking what I think you're thinking, are you?"

Alison's tone was guileless. "Probably, especially if you're thinking I'm in the market for a carpenter to renovate this house."

"You can't be serious!" Natalie screeched, scurrying from the window to stand in front of Alison's desk where she positioned her hands on either side of her waist.

Alison smiled with feigned innocence. "Why not?"

"Oh, Alison, be serious," June moaned, her happy face now pinched with worry.

"I am serious." Alison lifted her chin as she allowed her words to soak in.

"You're insane," Myra snapped.

"You mean you'd actually consider hiring a man like Rafe Beaumont to work for you?" It was Natalie who spoke this time, having joined the other women. They had formed a circle in front of Alison's desk.

Alison hesitated, but only briefly. "I might."

For a thunderous moment there was an air of suspended horror around the desk. Then Natalie and Myra spoke at once, each trying to make herself heard over the other.

"Why, that's the most ridiculous thing I've ever heard!"

"You wouldn't!"

Holding up her hand for silence, June cried, "Oh, honey, think of your reputation, if nothing else."

Suddenly realizing how ludicrous the entire conversation was, Alison threw back her head and laughed. "If anyone was listening, they'd think we were all nuts. Of course, I'm not going to hire Rafe Beaumont, but even if I were, it would be none of your business." When they would have interrupted, Alison hurried on, "But that's neither here nor there. I think we've raked that poor man over the coals long enough."

Pausing, she stepped from behind the desk. "If you'll remember, I invited you here to show you the house and fill you in on my plans. Now, are you interested or not?"

June sighed openly. "So, you really are hell-bent on going into business? There's nothing we can do to convince you that you ought to marry Arthur instead?"

Alison smiled. "Not a thing, dear friend. Once and for all, I'm not interested in remarrying. I'm interested in opening Silk Reflections and making a success of it. Now, are you ready for the tour?"

They followed quietly behind her as she left the room, her head high and her eyes flashing excitement.

Two days later, as Alison drove from her house to the site for her new store, the weather had turned colder and the sky was menacingly dark. The weather matched her mood perfectly. She stopped at the drugstore to pick up a bottle of aspirin. She'd been abusing them lately, taking a couple each night in hopes it would relax her so that she could sleep. Last night had been no exception.

Using a crutch, any crutch, she told herself, was ridiculous, but she couldn't stop. Every time she entered the house on Echo Lane, depression settled over her. The walls seemed to vibrate with emptiness. It seemed they took delight in mocking her. She missed Heather, missed her laughter, missed her bouncing up and down the stairs, missed their lengthy fireside chats. And she still missed Carter.

That was what had driven her out of the house and into the car. As usual, she was running, she realized as she skillfully steered the car back into the traffic. But thank goodness she had something to run to.

It wasn't because her marriage had been perfect that she felt this way. While far from perfect, it had been satisfactory and fulfilling.

Carter, reared as an only child by his father, his mother having died when he was in elementary school, had gained an independence early on, which he carried over into his home life as well as his business. After his father died, and he took over the family law firm, he more than doubled its success.

He had worked equally hard on making their relationship work, and she had enjoyed being married to him.

Nevertheless, she'd been sincere when she'd said she wasn't interested in a relationship with another man, especially with Arthur, though she knew he'd marry her in a heartbeat if she said the word.

Suddenly Rafe Beaumont's face flashed before her eyes, only to disappear as quickly. A frown marred Alison's smooth forehead. She hadn't thought of him since her friends had gone crazy with the gossip. As she'd told the girls, she was committed to her project and nothing else.

Now, as she braked the car in the drive of the rent house and got out, a gust of wind blew ragged leaves across her path, sending a chill through her.

Out of the corner of her eye she noticed that the lot next door was vacant. Then chastising herself for indulging in foolish fantasies, she hastily unlocked the door and stepped inside, the vacancy of the house rushing to meet her. However, it didn't impose the sort of numbness on her spirit as did the one on Echo Lane.

Immediately she went to the kitchen and fixed herself a cup of mocha coffee. After removing her windbreaker, she sat down at her desk, comfortable in jeans and an oversized blue sweater. She reached for her list of things to do and studied it carefully.

It seemed endless. If she was to meet her target date in January, it was imperative that she find someone qualified to do the renovation immediately.

It was while she was pondering which remodeling firm to try next—she'd already ruled out two—that she heard a noise coming from next door.

Dropping both the pencil and paper, Alison brought her head up with a start. Had Rafe Beaumont returned?

Fingering a loose strand of hair at the nape of her neck, Alison listened, then pushed herself away from the desk and walked to the window. At the sight of him, her heart did a crazy little flip-flop. He was again unloading material. She watched him awhile before spinning and walking back to her desk where she sat down again.

Moments later, failing to concentrate, she plunked her pencil down for the second time and leaned back in her chair.

"Why not?" she mused aloud.

After listening to her words rattle around in the silent room for a second, she grabbed her windbreaker and breezed out the door, slamming it behind her.

Three

Alison leisurely wound her way across the lawns that separated them, keeping her eyes on Rafe Beaumont, though she tried not to be obvious. She need not have worried about the latter. He was so busy he hadn't noticed her, or if he had, he wasn't letting on.

Drawing closer, she could see his profile; it was carefully defined. His pronounced jawline suggested stubbornness, but the nose was well shaped and blended into the craggy contours of his cheeks and the hard angle of his jaw. She was conscious of the strength he exuded, yet she experienced a tingle of fear along her back. Her study concluded with one word: dangerous, an exceedingly dangerous man to avoid at all cost.

Again he was wearing jeans, old and worn ones that hadn't held a crease in months, if ever, but that fit him like a glove. Fearing she would be caught staring where she shouldn't, Alison kept her eyes pinned above the waist. Even at that, she got more than she bargained for. His flannel work shirt, equally as worn, was open down the front, allowing her to see an abundance of wiry chest hair. She took a sudden breath.

Without warning, he raised his head and their eyes met. For an instant Alison had trouble breathing. She didn't realize until later that it was the glacier coldness of his eyes that robbed her of her breath.

He straightened to full height and leaned on the posthole digger. He was tall, taller than he'd first appeared, towering over her five foot six by at least eight inches. She found herself further captivated by the way he moved, like a well-honed athlete, effortless and graceful. He also had the body of one: halfback shoulders tapered to a flat stomach, trim hips and powerful thighs.

But the unrelenting coldness of his eyes continued to chill her to the marrow, though she didn't flinch under his stare. Suddenly feeling the need to say something, anything that would break the tension, she murmured inanely, "Hi."

He leaned more heavily on the tool and angled his head, wariness now replacing the coldness. "Hello."

Alison responded to the rich, deep timbre of his voice as quickly as she'd responded to him. She felt warm all over.

"It looks like we're going to be neighbors," she said haltingly, her face suffused with unnatural color.

He drew a sharp breath, and she was aware of him stiffening. "How do you figure that?"

Alison jammed her hands into the pockets of her jeans, momentarily disconcerted by the mocking edge in his voice and the bitterness now reflected in his eyes, a bitterness heightened by the grooves cut deeply around his mouth and across his forehead. None of those imperfections, however, detracted from his rough good looks; if anything, they enhanced them, merely making him appear older than he actually was. She mentally judged him to be around twenty-nine, which, if so, would make him six years her junior.

Even though she knew he was not overjoyed at being interrupted, there was nonetheless an unbridled curiosity in the wary gaze that was leveled on her.

Lifting her chin slightly, she said, "It's obvious you're setting up shop—" she dared not let on she knew what "—and since I am too, I thought—"

"You thought what?" he cut in.

Although her flush deepened, Alison refused to be put off by his abrupt manner. "I thought I'd introduce myself," she finished lamely.

"I see."

But he didn't. She was sure of that. The mocking glint in his eye along with his tone clearly said: Lady, what the hell are you doing here?

Which was a good question. What *was* she doing here, standing uncomfortably in front of him, trembling like some teenager on her first date? Rarely did she act on impulse. She always thought long and hard before she made a decision about anything. So what had possessed her to behave so irrationally?

Whatever the reason, it wasn't good enough to excuse her unorthodox behavior. What must he be thinking? Cringing inwardly, she lowered her eyes and concentrated on the spot of dirt on the end of one of her Reeboks.

"Look...Ms...."

At the sound of his voice, her head snapped up. "Alison Young," she said with a breathlessness she despised but was unable to control.

He didn't respond immediately. But with his eyes still on her, he shoved the tool aside and reached into his shirt pocket and pulled out a cigarette, along with a lighter. He flipped the lighter open, then hesitated. "Cigarette?"

She shook her head. "No thanks, I don't smoke."

"Wise choice," he replied, turning away, his impatience showing in the coiled stance of his body.

Alison swallowed a sigh as she watched his sensitive lips trap the cigarette between them, their line as masculine and well defined as the rest of him. A haze of blue-gray smoke flared between them. He stepped back and fanned the air, though no apology was forthcoming.

"I'm Rafe Beaumont," he said suddenly, unexpectedly, with a slight drawl, though his eyes remained cold.

"It's a pleasure to meet you."

He inclined his head, but didn't say anything.

She wasn't surprised. After all, this was her game; the next move was up to her. The wind tugged at her hair, loosening fine tendrils from the nape of her neck. She failed to notice, however, so intent was she in trying to figure out a way to retreat gracefully. She was determined not to make a bigger fool of herself than she already had.

"Look," she began a trifle breathlessly, "I'm...I'm sorry I bothered you."

"Why did you then?" he asked bluntly, his eyes on her mouth. "Were you curious? Is that what this is all about?"

Alison blinked. "Curious?"

"Yeah, curious. Curious as to what an ex-con looks like."

She gasped. "Are you always this rude, Mr. Beaumont?" Her tone was as cold as his eyes. What an insufferable man, she thought. When he still didn't say anything, she went on, "Or is it just me? If so, why don't you just tell me to get lost and be done with it?"

Her words seemed to stop Rafe in his tracks, and his gaze would have browbeat a lesser person. But Alison stood her ground, and another silence fell between them, thick and heavy.

"Look," he said at last, clearly uncomfortable. "It seems that somewhere along the line I lost the habit of civility."

She shook her head. "No, it's I who should apologize. I'm the one who invaded your—"

Rafe cut her off. "Are you planning on moving into the house?"

It took a moment for Alison's mind to switch gears. "No. Actually, I'm planning to turn it into a business."

He drew on his cigarette, then flicking it to the ground, crushed it with a booted foot. "A business, huh?"

"Hopefully after the first of the year I'll be selling silk flowers to the ladies of Monroe."

A ghost of a smile played havoc with the creases in his lean cheeks. "Well, I wish you luck."

If his rigid features hadn't eased, if he hadn't smiled—well, almost smiled—she would have said thank you, swung around and marched back where she came from. Instead she returned his smile, something clicking inside her, an emotion heretofore forgotten. She felt the sensation of heat rushing to the pit of her stomach. It had been a long time since a man had stirred her in such a way. But wasn't that why she was here?

Pushing that annoying question to the back of her mind, Alison smiled, her gaze drifting beyond his shoulder. "What are you building?"

Rafe's glance followed hers. "Stands." Turning back to face her, he went on, "I'm getting ready to sell Christmas trees—Virginia pines."

"I'm impressed," Alison said, thinking Myra's gossip turned out to be fact after all.

"Don't be. It's just another way to earn a living."

"Oh, but I am," she confessed cheerfully. "I envy anyone who has a talent for growing things. Let me anywhere near a live plant and it withers and dies."

"Maybe it's because you talk 'em to death," he said calmly.

At first the insult did not register, so carefully masked was it by his low, even tone. But then the

words hit their mark, and her lips separated partly
from surprise, partly from anger.

Her second thought was how to put him in his place.
But then, just as quickly as her temper had ignited, it
cooled. If he had come on to her as she had to him, she
would have put him in his place long before now. By
the same token, what right did she have to fault him
for doing the same to her? None. She had gotten exactly what she deserved. Amusement bubbled inside
her.

"Chalk that round up to you," she said without
rancor.

His brows lifted.

Her laughter broke through. "You're right, I do
have a big mouth."

Rafe cleared his throat and fidgeted, shifting from
one foot to the other. "Well, maybe I exaggerated a
little."

"We both know better, but it's nice of you to say
that anyway."

The grooves in his cheeks went slack, suggesting
amusement, but stopping short of a smile. "Whatever you say." His gaze was penetrating as if he was
trying his best to figure her out.

"Did—do you grow the trees yourself?" Even
though she knew the answer to that as well, she wanted
to hear him tell her.

Annoyance flickered across his face, and for a moment she thought he wasn't going to answer. So much
for the tiny truce, she thought.

"Actually my old man grew them. But he's dead
now, so it's left up to me," he said flatly, bitterly.

"I'm . . . I'm sorry about your dad," she said quietly.

"Don't be." His voice was tense with suppressed anger. "He drank himself to death."

This time it was Alison who didn't know what to say, so she didn't say anything.

As if suddenly realizing he'd been the one to say too much, Rafe leaned over and retrieved the hammer from the ground. When he straightened, the stern mask was once more in place, and he bore no resemblance to the man who had almost been human a few moments before.

A soft sigh split Alison's lips as their eyes unexpectedly met and held. Her pulse raced while a fine tension simmered in the air.

Rafe drove five fingers through his hair before averting his gaze.

"It's time I let you get back to work," she said, her mouth so dry she could hardly speak.

He faced her again, his forehead crisscrossed with frown lines. "Yeah, I guess so."

"Good luck with your trees."

"Thanks."

Alison gave him a lopsided smile before twisting around and heading toward the house. With every step she took, she felt his eyes boring into her back.

Shivering inwardly, she upped her pace.

Four

It was nearly dark by the time he began stacking lumber on the top shelf of the storeroom. And even though the breeze coming through the windows was brisk, it was pleasant, with a hint of burning leaves.

Rafe, however, paid scant attention to the weather, so intent was he on finishing his task and calling it a day. He had been up since sunrise. As soon as he'd finished in town, he'd come back to the farm where there had been another day's work waiting for him. Before he'd tackled the storeroom, he had marked the first crop of trees for cutting.

He was dog tired; every bone in his body ached. What he needed was a hot shower and a cold beer, though not necessarily in that order.

He lifted several two-by-fours and tried not to think about Alison Young. His efforts proved unsuccessful.

Beautiful. He'd never seen eyes the color of hers or skin so flawlessly smooth, or heard laughter so warm and husky. And her mouth, God, it was sensual, enticing. Just the thought of touching it set off a storm of passion inside him.

A lady. Always in control. Well almost, he thought with a humorless smile. The exception had been when he'd insulted her. Then she'd bristled, and for an instant that ladylike control had slipped, but only slightly. He rarely came in contact with women like her.

He had a theory that beautiful society women who were always in control had unexplored depths of passion hidden inside, and the right man could unleash those passions, sending them skyrocketing.

For a second he fantasized that he was that man, and she was beneath him, naked and hot. He went instantly and achingly hard. A twisted smile reshaped his lips.

"Sure thing, Beaumont, and a million dollar check's in the mail, too."

He jammed the wood on the shelf, berating himself for being such an idiot. Women like Alison Young weren't about to fraternize with white trash like him, especially white trash that had served time.

So why the hell had she come traipsing over to him? Curiosity. He'd accused her of it then, and he was certain of it now. After all, he was the talk of the town. No matter where he went, whispers followed.

"Why, that's Clyde Beaumont's no-account son. Heard he was back in town."

"How could he have the gall to come back after what he did?"

"Ah, you know them young folks nowadays—they got the gall of a government mule."

"What made him steal all them cars, anyway?"

"Heard he had a real bad home life."

"That ain't no excuse for stealing."

The gossip mongers were right; that wasn't any excuse for stealing. He grabbed another load of wood and once again jammed it on the shelf. He knew it was harmful to keep digging into the past, but there were times when the memories haunted him, and his thoughts dwelt on that terrible time in the pen.

It had been four years ago that he had walked out of prison a free man. By now he had hoped those long days and nights would have become only a fading memory. They hadn't. Those violent, empty days were still very much with him.

Looking back at the whole period, he knew he had never felt so insignificant, so worthless, so beaten down, so humiliated, so out of control.

He told himself he would never allow anything to make him feel like that again. Anything. Especially not a woman of Alison Young's caliber, a woman who was in a class that would never include him.

Yeah, she was beautiful, beautiful but dangerous. And the next time—if there was a next time—she sashayed herself across the lawn, he'd tell her to mind her own damned business.

"Planning to work till you drop?"

Rafe spun around, almost dropping the load in his arms. "Dammit, Tom, you scared the living hell out of me."

A short man with a bushy mustache and protruding belly limped across the threshold into the barnlike room, a grin plastered on his face. "Guess I did at that," he drawled, seemingly unperturbed by Rafe's hostile glare. "But then you were too busy giving that wood the devil to notice anything."

Rafe eyed Tom Lott, his friend and part-time helper, as he dragged his right leg behind him. He had almost lost the leg in a motorcycle accident, the leg that was now virtually no good to him.

"Wanna cigarette?" Rafe asked after a moment.

"Thought you'd never ask." Tom eased himself down onto an old cane-backed chair near Rafe, his rasping breath the only sound in the room.

The silence continued while both men drew long drags and contemplated the smoke that soon clouded the air.

Tom was the first to speak. "What's got your blood pressure over the boiling point? A second ago you looked mean enough to take on Mike Tyson and whip him."

"Ah, hell, it's nothing worth talking about," Rafe said grimly, leaning his back against a worktable.

"That so, huh?"

Rafe dropped the half-smoked Camel on the wooden floor and stepped on it. "One of these days I'm going to give up these foul things."

Tom chuckled. "Me, too. If I don't, Gayle's gonna kick me out."

"Speaking of Gayle, where is she?" Gayle was not only Tom's wife, but his best and only asset. She had stuck by Tom after the accident when he'd been unbearable to live with. She ran a small grocery she'd inherited from her father. Only in the last year had Tom taken interest in it again. Now, he not only worked in the nursery but he helped Rafe on the tree farm as well. And Rafe couldn't be more grateful or thankful.

"She's cooking," Tom finally responded between puffs. "That's why I stopped by, to invite you for dinner."

Rafe opened his mouth, only to have Tom hold up his hand. "Before you say no, she's cooking your favorite—chicken and spaghetti."

"Even so, I'm going to beg off. I'm not only beat, but I'm lousy company to boot."

"I won't argue that point."

"Thanks," Rafe muttered laconically, though a ghost of a smile appeared on his lips.

"Your sour mood wouldn't by any chance have anything to do with that good-looking blonde I saw you talking to earlier today?"

Rafe's head came up with a start. "How did you know about that?"

Tom shrugged. "Drove by with the intention of stopping, but when I saw you had company, I said what the hell, he doesn't need me."

"Oh, but I did," Rafe countered sarcastically, his brows coming together in a dark frown. "As you saw, I didn't get but two rows of stands up today."

Tom grinned. "Can't say that I blame you. With her around to—"

"Drop it, Tom."

"Aw, hell, humor me a little. At least tell me who she is and what she wanted."

"Sounds to me like you wanna know more than a little," Rafe muttered savagely.

Tom's grin widened, and Rafe responded with a disgusted snort.

"Well . . ." Tom prodded.

"Trust me, it's no big deal. But if it'll get you off my back, her name's Alison Young."

Tom whistled. "I knew I recognized her—just couldn't put a name to the face. That's Carter Young's widow. She's been in the store several times."

Rafe rubbed the back of his neck and scowled at his friend. For some inane reason he was shocked to learn she'd been married. She had looked so fragile, so untouched. . . .

"Okay, so what did she want?" Tom pressed, his tone mild compared to Rafe's.

"I figured she knew who I was and just wanted to see what an ex-con looked like."

Tom cursed loudly. "That's crap and you know it."

"Is it?"

"Hell, yes, it is," Tom replied flatly. "No one cares anymore."

"If that's so, then why do I get those condescending stares and hear whispers behind my back?"

"Because there's always gonna be some ignorant sonofabitches. You'll just have to ignore them."

"It's not that easy."

Tom pulled on the edges of his mustache. "Hell, I never said it was. But you're not the bad boy you make yourself out to be. Anyway, you paid for your mistake, and now you have a right to be treated fairly and left alone."

"You think anyone'll buy Christmas trees from me?"

"Sure do, especially since you're gonna have the best lookin' ones in town—and the best prices."

Rafe's lips thinned. "You know how I hated to come back to Monroe, but with the trees ready for harvest and Mother in the nursing home..."

"You had no choice," Tom finished for him, scratching his head. "Still you made the right one, too."

"I don't know," Rafe said with fierce conviction. "I still hate this town, and facing people—"

"Why? You don't have a thing to be ashamed of. You've been straight for years now, working your rear off. That oughta count for something."

"Yeah, only—"

"Ah, you're just feeling sorry for yourself, right?"

"Right."

"Why?" Tom demanded simply.

"Oh, hell, I don't know. I guess Alison Young stirred me up more than I want to admit."

Tom chuckled. "I can understand that. If I weren't so old and decrepit, I'd be stirred up, too. So, back to my original question. What did the lady want?"

"She's going to put a flower shop in the vacant house next to the lot."

"Mmm, now that sounds interesting." Tom cocked his head to one side and went on, "It's no secret her old man left her plenty. She's got more money than most folk got sense."

"Figures."

"Yeah, she's one classy lady." Tom scratched his head again. "Can't imagine why she'd want to work."

"Boredom would be my guess."

Tom sighed. "Ah, to have that problem."

"What else do you know about her?" Rafe asked nonchalantly.

Tom wasn't fooled. A slow, knowing grin spread across his face. "So you're interested after all."

Rafe turned red. "Go to hell," he muttered.

Tom slapped his knee and laughed. "All right, you made your point. Other than what I've already told you, I know that she has a younger sister who lives with her."

Rafe nodded and looked away.

As if sensing that Rafe had closed the subject, Tom slowly got to his feet. "Well, if you're going to be a horse's you-know-what and turn down my offer for dinner, I'll get outa your hair."

"Tell Gayle I'll take a rain check, okay?"

"I'll stop by the lot tomorrow and help you out."

"Good enough. See you then."

Just as Tom would have walked out the door, Rafe stopped him.

"By the way, thanks."

Tom waved his hand. "Think nothing of it. I owe you, remember?"

Later after he'd showered and eaten a bite, Rafe
stretched out on the couch and lay with his hands behind his head, Alison Young still very much on his
mind.

He was still smarting from the profound effect she
had had on him. The last thing he'd ever expected was
to set eyes on a woman and feel that he'd suddenly
been kicked in the gut. While he might want to ignore
that sensation, he could not. Like it or not, he was
smitten.

She's out of your league, Beaumont! Forget her!

He would, too. After all, tomorrow was another
day, and he had plenty of work to do. Nothing like
hard labor to keep one's mind on track. Without it he
wouldn't be worth killing.

He didn't want Alison Young messing around in his
mind. He would simply banish thoughts of her, not
dwell on her high, full breasts, shapely limbs and hair
that reminded him of bottled sunlight. As of this
minute she would cease to exist for him. Tonight.
Completely. Forever.

He wondered if he'd see her tomorrow.

Five

Damn!" Alison said, trying to balance the sack of groceries in one hand and close the door behind her with the other, all the while listening to the jarring ring of the telephone on the other side of the kitchen.

Quickly, she dropped the sack, only to watch in horror as it split, sending half the contents to the floor. Groaning, she raced toward the phone.

"Okay, okay, I'm coming," she muttered again, fairly certain it was Heather calling from Nacogdoches. If so, she didn't want to miss her call.

"Hello," she said, sounding short-winded.

"Alison?"

She relaxed, and after reaching for a nearby chair, sank into it. "Hi, Arthur."

"Is something wrong? You sound like you've been running."

She could see him in her mind's eye sitting at his desk at home, still impeccably dressed in a suit, his receding hairline shining in the lamplight. She almost smiled.

"Actually, I was just coming in from the grocery store. Had my hands full."

"I'm sorry. You want me to call you back?"

"No, no, that's all right."

"I don't suppose you've had dinner yet?" When Alison didn't answer, he went on, "Thought maybe you might like to try that new restaurant in Lufkin, then take in a movie."

Alison bit her lower lip in agitation. Spending an evening with Arthur did not appeal to her. She was tired and wanted to take a hot bath and go to bed.

"Oh, Arthur, thanks, but no thanks. Not tonight. I'm bushed. I've been poring over catalogs all day."

"How's it coming?"

"So far so good, except that I'm probably not going to open on time. There's just so much to do."

Before today, Arthur was the only person she had told about the shop, but since he handled her business affairs, she had had no choice but to inform him. Though he hadn't been exactly enthusiastic, he hadn't criticized her, which in itself was something.

"You'll do it. I have confidence in you."

"Thanks. You know how much I count on your support."

"Well, if you're not going to dinner, I won't keep you."

"I'm glad you called," she said sincerely.

"When am I going to see you?"

Alison suppressed a deep sigh. "Soon, I promise."

"I'll hold you to that. Good night."

Thrusting thoughts of Arthur aside was as easy as replacing the receiver, though a persistent, nagging guilt lingered. She wished she could love Arthur. Shaking her head, she turned to the task of putting away the groceries.

Once that task was complete, Alison made her way into the huge den. The room was her favorite, open and spacious with two walls of glass doors and windows opening out onto the deck and swimming pool, and a stone fireplace in one corner. Tonight, however, she didn't linger in front of the burning fire that her maid had started before she left, opting to go straight to her bedroom.

The moment she opened the door and stepped inside, the emptiness, the loneliness struck her like a slap in the face. In this room it seemed to take on a lifelike quality.

She blamed her melancholy on the upcoming holiday season and the memories it awakened. She really should consider selling the house and moving into a condo, especially with her starting to work. Still it was home to both her and Heather, and she couldn't bring herself to part with it, even though she sometimes cursed it.

Refusing to feel sorry for herself, Alison discarded her clothes and padded naked into the bathroom. Minutes later she was out of the shower and rubbing herself with lotion. It was while she was massaging her body that she found herself thinking, inexplicably, about Rafe Beaumont.

"Oh, Lord," she groaned aloud. "Not him again."

With her face suddenly flushed, Alison donned a robe and charged out of the bathroom. She didn't stop until she was back in the den. But the minute she sat down and closed her eyes, she knew she hadn't out-run her thoughts.

Whatever had compelled her to cross the yard and introduce herself to that man still mystified her as well as embarrassed her. Had Rafe been right? Had it been curiosity, not because he was an ex-con, as he'd charged, but because she'd wanted to see if he looked as good up close as he had from afar?

Or closer to the truth, had she been curious to see if she could still attract a good-looking man, a good-looking *younger* man? So was sex what her attraction to Rafe was all about, what had stirred those wanton feelings inside her? Just a craving to be touched, to be kissed in a frenzy of physical gratification?

Suddenly furious with the mental game she was playing, she flounced off the couch and stormed across the room to the desk in the corner. She had her hand on a stack of catalogs when the doorbell chimed.

Relief surged through her, and she dropped the catalogs and dashed toward the door. It wasn't until she had her hand on the knob that she wondered who would be visiting her at eight o'clock at night.

"Who is it?" she asked hesitantly.

"Open up, sis, I'm freezing."

With a happy cry, Alison unbolted the door and jerked it open.

"Heather, what on earth?"

Laughing, Heather Phillips breezed across the threshold.

"Surprised, huh?"

Alison looked at her sister and smiled, thinking again how lovely she was. Taking after their mother, she was tall and slender with dark hair and dark eyes. Alison had wanted Heather to be a model, and after graduating from high school, Heather had indulged her for a year, then decided modeling was not for her. Several months later she enrolled in Stephen F. Austin State University where she was now a marketing major.

"You most certainly did surprise me," Alison said at last, reaching over and giving her sister another kiss on the cheek. "But I'm delighted, though I can't imagine what brings you home in the middle of the week."

"Nothing, really. Nancy Frazier left some papers here last weekend, and when she told me she was driving home to get them, I asked if I could tag along. My first class in the morning isn't until ten."

"Well, you know I'm always glad to see you." Alison's lips curved downward. "Old habits die hard. I still wake up thinking I need to get you up so you won't be late for school."

Heather laughed. "You ought to be glad you don't have to get up so early anymore."

"I get up anyway, so I'd just as soon you were here," Alison told her as they linked arms and walked into the kitchen. Heather dumped her large bag on the buffet table and sat down.

"Want something to drink?" Alison asked.

"Hot chocolate sounds good."

"What I really wish," Alison said, standing in front of the microwave, "is that SFA was closer, so you could commute."

Heather was silent while she reached for the cup. "Me, too. At least sometimes," she qualified. "Most of the time I enjoy the hubbub of campus life."

"I know you do, and that's really where you belong. It's just selfishness on my part to still want you home. Anyway, I'd worry about you being on the road all the time."

Heather grinned. "Ah, admit it, sis, you worry anyway." Her grin suddenly faded, and she reached out and grabbed Alison's hand. "I know you miss me and that you're lonely, but it's because you choose to be. Arthur would marry you in a minute, only—"

"Only I won't marry him," Alison finished for her. "Wasn't that what you were going to say?"

Heather nodded.

"Well, you're right, I won't." Alison smiled, taking the sting out of her tone.

"But if you did, you wouldn't be so lonely."

"Maybe, maybe not."

Heather rolled her eyes.

"What about you, young lady? It's time you found yourself a—"

"I think maybe I have," Heather said, flashing a grin.

Alison was stunned, and it showed.

"Close your mouth, sis dear. You heard right. I'm seeing someone."

"As in dating, you mean?"

Heather rolled her eyes again. "That's kind of an old-fashioned term, but yes, that's what I mean."

"Do I know him?"

"You sure do," Heather said, her eyes sparkling.

"Ah, now I'm finding out the real reason you came home."

Heather's grin was sheepish. "Well, that's part of it."

"All right, who is he?"

"Tim Merrill."

"Juanita and Jack's son?"

"Yes." Some of the animation left Heather's face, and she added hurriedly, "I know you don't like Juanita, but—"

"Of course I like her," Alison inserted quickly, "it's just that she's a—"

"Snob." Heather giggled over the rim of her cup. "Go ahead and say it."

"Well," Alison said with a reluctant smile, "it's just that she has more money than most and likes to flaunt it."

"Like your friend Myra, right?"

Alison raised an eyebrow at Heather's astuteness. "Right. But Tim's a fine young man, and if you're happy that's all that counts."

Heather got up and walked to the sink to set her cup down. When she turned back around and faced Alison, her eyes were serious. "I'm happier than I've ever been, so keep your fingers crossed."

Alison smiled sweetly. "That goes without saying."

"Well, if it's all the same to you, I'll say good-night. I've got a zoo test tomorrow afternoon that's going to be a dilly."

"Before you go," Alison said quietly, "there's something I want to tell you."

"What is this?" Heather quipped. "A night for confessions?"

"It's a surprise, sort of."

"I'm listening."

Alison hesitated, but only briefly. "I'm going to work."

Heather frowned. "Work. Are you serious?"

"Very."

"But why?"

"Why not?" Alison countered gently.

Heather gave a nonchalant shrug, but Alison wasn't fooled. She knew she was upset; the white line around her lower lip was the giveaway.

"But...but you're so busy with your charity work," Heather stammered, "and the women's shelter." She paused and spread her hands. "Besides, you love to play bridge and tennis."

"Oh, honey, those things are simply not enough anymore."

"So what are you going to do?" Heather asked, averting her gaze.

Alison told her about Silk Reflections.

Heather gnawed on her bottom lip. "What about the house? Will you sell it and move into town?"

Alison saw the apprehension, the fear lurking behind those huge, dark eyes, and her heart turned over. Even though Heather was twenty, she was both immature and insecure. And spoiled. Alison took the blame for all three. When their parents died, the bottom had dropped out of Heather's world. It had taken her and Carter years to reconstruct it.

"Sis?"

The anxious tone in Heather's voice tore at Alison. "Oh, honey, of course I'm not going to sell the house," she said in her most reassuring tone. "And on weekends I'll still be here for you, even if I have to get someone to work for me on Saturdays."

The color quickly returned to Heather's face, though she seemed to have a hard time meeting Alison's eyes. "You . . . you think I'm awful, don't you?"

Alison smiled. "Not awful, just a little spoiled."

"I'll have to admit that you're talented—you can work miracles with your hands."

Alison stood, her gaze anxious. "Is that your way of saying you approve?"

Heather grinned sheepishly. "Guess so."

Laughing, Alison closed the distance between them and hugged her tightly.

Six

The day had promised to be a splendid one.

Upon awakening Alison had dashed to the window and opened the miniblinds to a sun eking over the horizon. Eager to get the day started, she had dressed hastily in cream-colored slacks and a tangerine V-necked sweater.

But now, two hours later, as she maneuvered the car in the direction of the rent house, she tried to make light of her first disappointment. She had just gotten Heather up and off to SFA when the phone rang. It was June canceling their weekly luncheon date. Having already packed finger sandwiches, a container of fresh chicken salad, wine and cheese, she'd said to hell with it and walked out the door, hamper in tow. June or no June, she'd dine alone at the house and enjoy it.

The second she rounded the corner onto Maple Street, she saw him. And much to her chagrin, her heart upped its beat.

By the time she parked the car and slipped from under the wheel, she noticed the palms of both hands were moist.

"Oh, for heaven's sake, Alison!"

Chastising herself aloud seemed to have the desired effect, because when she started up the walkway, she was once again in control—no erratic heartbeat, no sweaty palms.

Rafe was working on the end of the lot closest to her, and was dressed in his usual worn jeans and flannel shirt, this one a blue and green plaid. Though he was busy hammering, she knew he'd seen her. Yet he didn't pause in his work.

Instantly, she rebelled. How dare he ignore her? She shouldn't let his rudeness get to her, but it did. Deciding she wasn't going to let him get away with his surly manner, she strolled casually to the door and just after she inserted the key into the lock, she angled her head and cut her eyes toward Rafe. The wind had ruffled the dark strands of his hair, adding to his shaggy disheveled look, a look she'd decided suited his appearance perfectly.

For all the notice he gave her, however, she could have been invisible. Determined more than ever to dent that armor he wore so proudly, she said with false sweetness, "Good morning, Mr. Beaumont."

At the sound of her voice, his head came up and around.

Their eyes met, and Alison bristled anew at the impatience she saw flare in his. But there was something else, another emotion, so fleeting that she couldn't identify it. Was it blatant hostility? Or hot desire?

Instinctively, she knew that even a mild association with a man like Rafe Beaumont could only lead to trouble. Despite that danger, she couldn't turn away. An awareness, an electricity she had never felt before, sparked between them.

"Morning," he finally drawled, his voice laced with cynicism.

Suddenly unable to decide if she was more miffed with herself or with him, Alison smiled tightly, then walked through the door without a backward glance.

Pushing that unsettling encounter to the back of her mind, she attacked her work with a vengeance. But the lovely morning seemed tarnished somehow. Though she worked up several orders and made numerous phone calls to companies she was interested in doing business with, she was restless.

By the time her grumbling stomach forced her to stop and look at her watch, she felt as though she had fought a battle and lost. Muttering a curse, she pushed away from the desk, walked to a nearby closet and pulled out a card table and chairs. Then remembering that June wasn't coming, she shoved the extra chair back against the wall.

Because of the bright sunshine, though it did little to temper the nip in the air, Alison set the table up in front of the window overlooking the backyard, which she hoped would soon be a parking lot.

Once she'd placed the tablecloth on the table and set out the food, she sat down, but instead of immediately satisfying the gnawing in her stomach, she gazed outside again. The ceiling-to-floor window afforded an uninterrupted view of the lawn that stretched to a thicket of sweet gum and Chinese tallow trees. Beyond, tall red oak towered above neighboring rooftops, their patches of color almost blinding beneath a cloudless sky.

Twisting slightly, she caught Rafe in her line of vision. He had pulled down the tailgate of his truck and was perched on the end of it, sipping from a cup. After a moment he stood, pitched the remaining contents on the ground and sauntered back toward his tools.

Alison stood as well, knowing what she was going to do before her gaze once again swept wistfully over the plentiful display of food on the table.

All he can say is no, she told herself, striding purposefully out the door. Refusing to think further about her actions, Alison kept her head down until she was nearly upon him.

"Now what, Ms. Young?" he said curtly.

She raised her head and stopped in her tracks. And stared. He was in the process of taking off his shirt.

"I...I thought you might be—" She broke off, the remainder of the sentence sticking in her throat. Then swallowing, she asked inanely, "What are you doing?"

"What does it look like I'm doing?" he drawled.

Positive that he was aware of her sudden confusion and discomfort, Alison felt a flurry of resentment.

However, her heightened agitation seemed merely to egg him on. He worried over each button, while his eyes held hers captive.

Alison didn't know whether to turn her head or to run. She did neither. To her dismay, she stood rooted to the spot, his hot stare ripping her nerves to pieces.

"You were saying?" There was a mocking challenge in his tone as he slowly finished unbuttoning his shirt and peeling it off.

Alison had expected the full exposure of his chest and his stomach to affect her, but not to such an extent. Stone-hard and flat, it brought on a flush of desire so intense her insides flamed.

Reflectively, she moistened her lips. There was no sound except her heartbeat, which she thought was thunderous.

Damn him. He had become an obsession, interfering with her work, creeping into her thoughts when least expected.

"Look, Ms. Young," he said into a silence that was threatening to explode, "is this visit just a replay of yesterday, or what?"

"No."

"Then what's the deal?" He sounded tired.

Outwardly she appeared calm, though inwardly she was a mess. "The deal is an invitation to share lunch with me."

Rafe stared at her in stunned disbelief, then threw back his head and laughed, a deep belly laugh that totally lacked in humor. "Jeez, you're something else, lady. Now why would you want to do a thing like that?''

Before she could answer, he turned and tossed his wadded-up shirt into the bed of his pickup. It was then that she saw it, saw the jagged scar that crisscrossed from under his left armpit down to his waist.

If she hadn't clamped down on her lower lip, she would have gasped aloud. Still something must have communicated her horror to him, for he spun back around, his eyes narrowed into slits.

"Not a pretty sight, is it, Ms. Young?'' he taunted harshly.

Alison wet her lips before lifting horrified eyes up to him. "Where...did...?''

"Prison, Ms. Young,'' he lashed out, "that's where.''

"You mean someone did that to you?''

He laughed mirthlessly. "I sure as hell didn't do it to myself.''

"How...how did it happen?'' Alison asked, her face ashen.

"A sonofabitch stole up on my blind side and tried his damndest to spill my guts on the floor.''

If it was his intent to shock, he'd hit the mark. Her stomach revolted at the unvarnished truth. To think that a knife had plunged into his skin and ripped it open...

"Oh, God,'' she said in a throaty voice she hardly recognized as her own, unable to tear her eyes off the grotesque scar.

"Now tell me you still want me to have lunch with you?" he sneered, stepping closer, looming over her.

Alison didn't flinch, nor did she back down from the challenge reflected in his eyes. "I still want you to have lunch with me."

She knew she had shocked him, though he took great pains to hide it. There was a flicker in his eyes, a flicker of confusion that she hadn't missed. He had expected her to be repulsed, to bolt like a frightened doe.

He gave her a wry smile. "Just exactly what kind of game are you playing?"

"I'm not playing a game, Mr. Beaumont," she said evenly. "A friend stood me up. I have more food than I'll ever eat." Eager to put things back on an even keel, Alison smiled.

Suddenly his stern features relented, and he reached for his shirt. "Let's go."

Seven

Few words passed between them as he sat across from her. The number of finger sandwiches and spoonfuls of chicken salad he consumed was certain to qualify for *The Guinness Book of Records*.

She could find no fault with his manner, however. He ate as if he relished it, and the food simply disappeared.

"Are you ready for more sandwiches?" she asked, her mouth slanted in a small smile. "I have plenty."

He stopped eating and looked directly at her, his blue eyes piercing. "What about yourself? You've hardly touched your food."

"I...rarely eat much for lunch," she replied, her voice husky for no apparent reason.

But there was a reason; she simply didn't want to acknowledge it. She was too busy staring—at his chest. Again. She had tried not to, but she couldn't help it. When he had put his shirt back on he'd left it unbuttoned halfway, and she was conscious of nothing but the leathery browned skin that was exposed.

Swallowing a sigh, Alison took a bite of the chicken salad while he finished what was on his plate. She laid down her fork. "You care for anything else?" she asked politely.

She had to say something; she'd endured the silence as long as she could, though it didn't seem to bother him.

He glanced up from his plate. "Thanks, but I couldn't down another morsel. I don't know when I've eaten this much."

"I'm glad you enjoyed it."

"I certainly did that," he said, pushing his plate away.

"You always eat this much?"

The curve of his lips suggested a smile. "So you think I ate a lot, huh?"

She laughed, and at the same time their eyes met. The connective force of their gaze was palpable. Blood rushed through her head, and behind it came the pounding of her heart.

To diffuse the dangerous tension, Alison reached for his plate and left the room. When she returned from the kitchen, carrying two cups of coffee, he was staring outside.

"I don't mind if you smoke," she said quietly, placing one cup in front of him before sitting back down.

He acknowledged the coffee with a nod, then said, "Thanks, but I'm trying to swear off the nasty things."

Sipping his coffee, he seemed utterly relaxed and without a care. She found this calmness as unexpected as she did comforting.

However, she wasn't deceived. She remembered his eyes of a while ago, how they had cut through her like slivers of glass, only to then soften, like they were now.

But the anger was still there, hidden just beneath the surface. She'd been on the receiving end of it and didn't mean to be again. It frightened her, but heaven help her, it excited her as well.

Rafe sighed suddenly, impatiently. It was sufficient to roust her out of her thoughts.

"You're a good cook; the man in your life is lucky."

His casual comment stunned Alison so that for a minute she couldn't think of a suitable answer.

"I'm a widow, Mr. Beaumont," she said stiffly.

"I know."

Again he caught her off guard. "Oh." The tiny word was more a question than a statement.

"Need I remind you that this is a small town?"

"Hardly," she said defensively. "What else do you know about me?"

His answer was nonchalant. "Nothing, except you have a sister who's your responsibility and you married into an old and aristocratic family." He paused.

"And that you don't have to worry about where your next meal is coming from."

Alison's eyes darkened with disapproval. She was tempted to put him in his place, only to remember hearing Myra say how poverty-stricken he'd been. Apparently he hadn't always known where his next meal was coming from. Her anger drained away.

"Anything more?" she asked, drawing in a ragged breath.

He shook his head, turning away.

"What about you, Rafe?"

She couldn't be sure whether it was the use of his name or the question that caused him to twist around so suddenly.

"What about me?" he asked, on guard.

"Have you ever been married?"

He barked a hollow laugh. "Nope, never found a woman who wanted to marry an ex-con. But then I suspect you know far more about me than I do about you. Don't think I'm not aware that the tongues are wagging hot and heavy about me."

Color flooded her face. "Well, I'll admit there's been talk—"

He winced as if her words had struck a nerve. "That's exactly why I didn't want to come back to Monroe."

"Why did you, then?" she asked softly.

"I had no choice. When my old man died, there was no one to look after the farm...or my mother." He paused and expelled a harsh breath. "She's in a nursing home, brain-dead from a stroke, but then I guess you knew that, too."

His words caught her unaware, and for a crazy moment she longed to comfort him. Instinct told her he wouldn't appreciate her sympathy. "No, I didn't know that, and I'm sorry."

"Yeah, so am I," he muttered, his expression closed.

"You mentioned the farm," she said hastily, groping for a subject that would remove the stark pain from his eyes. "What are your plans for it?"

He looked at her for a long moment, and his gaze raked her body.

Alison had decided to wear her hair loose today, giving it free rein to curl riotously around her head and shoulders. Trying desperately to diffuse the mounting tension, she raised an arm and thrust her hand through the unruly mass. When she did, it created a deep gap at the neck of her sweater.

Instantly, she heard his sharp intake of breath and saw his gaze fall to the valley between her breasts. For what seemed no longer than a heartbeat, he stared at the creamy skin that was exposed, his expression unreadable. Only the bobbing up and down of his Adam's apple showed he was disturbed.

Alison's breath started to rasp in her throat, and at the same time her nipples hardened. Feeling the situation getting out of control, she quickly averted her gaze.

The moment was shattered.

"Do you really want to know about the farm, or are you just making polite conversation?" His tone held a trace of mockery.

She faced him again, her chin raised a notch. "I really want to know."

"Okay, I plan to turn it into a tree farm, exclusively."

"In other words, you're going to forget cattle and vegetables."

"Right. At the moment, I have a thousand Christmas trees ready to be shipped."

Her eyes widened. "I had no idea. Why, that's a business in itself, isn't it?"

"No, unfortunately it isn't," Rafe said. "Raising Christmas trees can be good supplemental income for small landowners like myself, but it'll never take the place of my carpentry work."

"That's too bad."

"You're right, especially since tree farming is so damned much work. It takes four years from planting to harvest, and in between we have to battle deer, pigweeds and pine tip moths."

"Pigweeds?" Alison frowned. "Sounds awful."

His amused, tolerant smile told her that he wasn't surprised by her reaction. "Could be worse, I guess. Mother Nature not cooperating, for instance. One swoop of bad weather can do your crop in."

Alison was thoroughly fascinated by what he was telling her, and it was obvious he was in his element. He had completely dropped his guard, his voice tempered with enthusiasm. And during it all, she tried to dwell on what he was saying and not how attractive he was.

"So what's the secret to keeping them healthy?"

"Spraying the hell out of them, that's what. In addition, they have to be pruned, and that takes a lot of my free time."

"But if the trees are gorgeous, I guess it's worth it."

"You bet it's worth it," Rafe said, reaching for his cup and lifting it to his lips.

Alison watched a moment in silence as his tanned hand circled the fine china. "I can't imagine what's so special about a tree that inspires such tireless devotion."

Rafe shrugged. "I guess it's that same special something that's urging you to go into the flower business, even though you don't have to work."

"You're right, of course." Excitement edged Alison's voice. "I love working with my hands, taking a bunch of flowers and arranging them into a masterpiece. But trees—why, they're just that, trees."

Rafe's lips twisted. "Have you ever seen a Virginia pine?"

"No, I don't think so."

"Well, you'll just have to see one to believe."

"Maybe I will," she said casually.

"Maybe you will."

Did he mean it? she asked herself, taking advantage of the quiet to search his features. It was hopeless; he gave nothing away. She averted her gaze then, positive they were both simply making courteous conversation that was meaningless the moment it was spoken. Still, she was curious.

Rafe cleared his throat, drawing her gaze back to his. When their eyes met again, she had no trouble reading the expression this time. Her heart sank. Like quicksilver, his mood had changed.

"Now suppose you tell me what this is all about?" he demanded in a cold, flat voice. "Why did you invite me here to lunch? We both know it's not because you're starved for the company of the opposite sex, nor was it to make small talk."

"There's no reason to be insulting." Alison's anger was hardly subtle.

"Like hell there isn't!"

She felt the tension climb as they stared at each other like two enemies quietly sizing each other up. Gone was the rapport of a moment ago. Hostility was back in the grim set of his features.

"Look, I don't know what kind of smoke you're blowing up my nose, but—"

Alison let out a rush of air. "I'd like you to work for me."

Nothing about him changed, except the blue eyes that instantly iced over. "Why?"

Her tongue probed her upper lip. "I thought that would be obvious—I need a carpenter to renovate this house."

"Why me?"

"Why not you?"

He muttered a blistering expletive. Alison winced, but didn't say anything.

"Off the top of my head, I can think of a dozen reasons."

Alison refused to back down. "You said yourself that the trees were only a side venture, that you had to work."

"Dammit, I know what I said, but—"

"But what? If you don't need the work, then feel free to turn me down."

"You're not afraid of me?"

"Should I be?"

"Of course not," he muttered savagely.

"Then—"

He didn't let her finished the sentence. "How do you know that I'm trustworthy?"

She sighed. "Are you?"

"Yes, but how do you know I'll do a good job?"

"Will you?"

"Yes," he said again, staring at the ceiling, a vein in his jaw pulsing rapidly. "Only it's not that simple," he added, bringing his eyes back level with hers. "What about your reputation? Bet you never thought about that."

"That's not your worry," Alison said stubbornly. "It's mine."

"Yeah."

"So what's your answer?" she asked, ignoring his sarcasm.

Rafe's eyes were thorough in their close study of her, as if he was trying to figure out what made her tick. Then he lifted his gaze heavenward. "I must be out of my mind, but what the hell. All right, I'll do it."

Refusing to acknowledge the sudden fluttering in her stomach, Alison stood. "Good," she said in her most businesslike tone. "Come on, I'll show you what I want done."

"I can't get started right away," he said, stalling her. "The Christmas trees have to be taken care of first."

"That's fine. I'm willing to wait."

He looked at her for another long moment, then shaking his head, he pushed the chair back and got up.

The house, though old, was in fairly good condition, with the exception of a back porch that ran the entire length of the house. The other rooms consisted of three small bedrooms, two baths, living room, dining room, and kitchen.

"I'd like the living room filled with shelves and display cabinets, along with two of the bedrooms," Alison explained as they walked the premises. "The back bedroom I had in mind for an office." She paused and looked up at him. "Well, what do you think?"

They were in the kitchen now, and Rafe was standing so close to her that she could smell the faint aroma of his cologne. A soft sigh trembled from her as she purposefully placed distance between them.

Her sudden movement hadn't gone undetected. His features darkened, and when he spoke, his voice was tight. "No problem. It can be done, but it's going to cost you a bundle with materials being what they are."

"I know."

"What about the porch? Any plans for it?"

She frowned. "It's in such bad shape, my first thought is to say tear it off."

"What about a workroom? Don't you need one?"

"I thought I would use my office for that."

"I hardly think it's large enough. Let's have a look at the porch."

The moment Rafe opened the kitchen door, Alison smelled the musty dampness. She paused on the threshold. "I hate coming out here."

Rafe, having stepped in front of her, looked around. "I can understand why. This place is a mess, but all is not lost. I can fix it."

Alison doubted that. As far as she was concerned it was a total loss. Not only was the wood on the floor buckling, but it sagged in the middle like a piece of wet cardboard. The ceiling was also in sad need of repair. It had rotted and looked as if it could come crashing down anytime. Folding her arms across her chest, she shivered.

"Cold?" Rafe asked, turning to face her.

"A little."

"Why don't you go back inside? I'll only be a minute."

"I'm all right," Alison said, following as he walked deeper into the porch.

"What's in there?" Rafe asked, pointing toward a large, wooden cabinet that occupied one end of the room.

"Probably nothing but junk. The last tenants left it here, and I haven't taken the time to have it hauled off."

"Mmm, it'd make you a dandy storage closet," Rafe remarked, stepping forward and reaching for the handle.

Within seconds after the door swung back on its hinges, Alison froze, then let out a bloodcurdling scream.

Eight

What the hell!'' Rafe shouted, whipping around, his face stricken.

Alison, shaking like a leaf in a windstorm, stared at him with glazed eyes. "Oh, God, Rafe, a...a...." She stopped, taking deep, gulping breaths, her eyes on the floor. "Oh, God," she wheezed again, "is...it gone?"

Rafe took a tentative step toward her. "Is what gone?" When she didn't answer, his voice rose, "For god's sake, Alison, what are you talking about? Tell me what's wrong!"

She licked her parched lips. "When...when you opened that door, a...a rat ran across my foot and—" Again she broke off, unable to go on, huge tears trickling down her cheeks.

Rafe simply stared at her for several seconds, his mouth open, as if she'd completely taken leave of her senses. "A rat? You saw a rat? Is that what this is all about?"

"It . . . it touched me," Alison whimpered. "It ran across my foot."

Rafe stared at her another moment. Then he laughed, laughed with sincere delight that came from the heart; there was nothing phony about it. When he could talk again, he said, "You mean you got all bent out of shape over a rat? Hell, woman, I thought something terrible had happened." He gave his neck a savage rub. "You scared the bloody—"

"How dare you laugh at me!" Alison cried, glaring at him, exciting a fresh onslaught of tears. "I don't see what's so funny! Anybody would've screamed."

As if it finally dawned on Rafe exactly how upset she was, the remaining scraps of amusement on his face disappeared. "Hey, lighten up, it's okay. It was only a rat." He stepped closer, the lines on his face loosening a bit.

"Stay away from me!" Alison said, backing up.

A stinging curse whistled through his lips, but it was lost on Alison. On legs that had the consistency of melted butter, she spun and charged for the door, determined to put as much distance between her and Rafe as possible.

"Alison!"

She paid him no heed.

He tore after her.

Trembling violently and unable to control it, Alison upped her pace and stepped into the kitchen, her breath coming in short rasps.

"Dammit, woman!"

He reached her just as her toe struck a piece of linoleum sticking up from the floor, and she lost her balance.

"Oh!" Alison cried, watching as the floor rose to meet her, powerless to do anything about it.

"Don't worry, I have you." Rafe's firm, steady voice came from behind.

The voice did nothing to reassure her; it was the strong arms that circled her shoulders that were her salvation.

Groaning, Alison let him bear the brunt of her weight, only to then realize her mistake.

"Damn!" Rafe hissed as his legs buckled and folded beneath him, carrying him forward. Simultaneously, their knees hit the hard, cold floor with a thunk.

Feeling a sharp jolt of knifelike pain, Alison moaned, slinging her arm around Rafe's waist and hanging on as if her life depended on it. With her fingers digging into his waist, Rafe's free arm found its way under her rib cage. Fighting to regain his balance and hold on to her at the same time, he sank a hand into the soft side of her breast.

They froze.

For several seconds, neither knew what do say, what to do, what not to do. Their breaths hung in the air. Alison, aware of a different kind of pain now, closed her eyes tightly and waited for the heat to stop flowing from her breast to the rest of her body.

Because she was still nestled against him, it took her by surprise when Rafe moved, causing his shirt to come loose from his jeans. Instantly her fingers came in contact with his warm, hard skin. Her eyes rounded as she looked up at him. The moment was airless. She could hear his heartbeat; it was as loud as her own.

His lips were so close now that she could almost taste his breath as it whispered against her parted lips, caressing her, tempting her. She ached to feel his mouth against hers. It was that craving, that fierce hunger that shook her, that forced her into action.

Stiffening, she whispered, "Rafe . . . please."

He seemed to be as stunned as she was, and for several ponderous seconds he couldn't move or speak.

Time seemed to limp past.

Then he straightened, pulling her up with him. "You okay?" he asked hoarsely, dropping his arms to his sides.

"I'm . . . fine," she said with a shaky laugh that brought a touch of color to her cheeks.

He stared at her in a glazed way. "You sure?"

The frenzy had left; the raw feeling had been disguised. But now that they were upright and on steady ground, Alison was mortified, so mortified she wished the floor would open up and swallow her. With burning cheeks, she stammered, "I'm...sure. What about you, are you all right?"

Rafe took a long time to respond. "Don't worry about me."

"I'm sorry, I didn't mean—" she began.

He waved his hand, cutting her off. "Forget it. I have." Though he showed no outward emotion,

Alison knew he was as on edge as she was; his voice sounded strained, as if his throat had closed.

There was a moment of heavy silence, then he asked, "Tell me, you always react to varmints like that?"

Pallor replaced the heightened color in Alison's cheeks. "I don't know which I hate worse, rats or roaches," she said, shivering again.

His voice, though still pitched low, sounded almost normal. "I advise you to get an exterminator in here first thing tomorrow."

"Don't worry, I will."

Another silence ensued, more awkward than the one before, during which each went to great lengths to make sure their eyes never made contact.

After a moment Rafe said, "If there's nothing else to discuss right now, I'd best be going back to work."

"Of course," Alison murmured politely, trying desperately to put things back on an even keel. But it was impossible, especially with Rafe's eyes resting on her again, not casually, but seriously, as though he was searching for answers when there were no questions.

"I'll put something on paper and give it to you in the next day or so."

He continued to stare at her unwaveringly, but she avoided looking at him. "That'll be fine."

"I'll see you later."

Alison followed him to the door. Once there he turned, and this time she couldn't avoid his dark gaze. "Thanks for lunch."

"You're welcome," she said, well aware of the rapid beat of her pulse.

When he closed the door behind him, Alison sank against it and took a deep, shuddering breath. She was shaky inside. And scared. But alive, more alive than she'd ever been in her life.

Rafe had dreaded coming home. He could have gone to Tom and Gayle's, he reminded himself, stopping the truck in front of the house and killing the engine. They would have welcomed him with open arms, offered him a cold beer and a hot dinner. Visiting the nursing home had also been an alternative.

He hadn't given either more than a flicker of a thought because he wasn't fit company for himself, much less anyone else. He wasn't about to inflict his foul humor on his friends, or his mother for that matter, not that she would notice the difference, he thought dejectedly.

Although it was only six o'clock and barely dark, Rafe felt that it should be bedtime. He was just that tired. He knew it would be an effort to haul his body out of the truck.

When he'd left Alison and gone back to the lot, he'd worked like a man possessed, determined to take out his frustrations on the wood. And he had, finishing the stands and setting them up. He'd quit only after he'd smashed the end of one of his fingers. It had hurt so badly, he'd nearly fainted.

He'd rounded up his tools, and without so much as a glance in the direction of 123 Maple, he'd headed home.

Wearily, he climbed out of the truck and walked up on to the porch. He had the front door open and was about to step inside when he heard the whine behind him, followed by a loud thumping sound.

Rafe lowered his head, not at all startled by what he saw. A large, black-haired dog was sitting on his hind legs, peering up at him with wide, sad eyes, his head cocked to one side.

"Hey, fellow," Rafe said, bending over and scratching the dog behind the ears. "So you're back again, huh?"

As if understanding him, the dog sought his hand with a warm, wet tongue.

Grinning, Rafe stood. "All right, you can come in, and I'll feed you. But if you run away again, you've had it. Understand? No more free vittles."

Again the dog cocked his head and whined, as if he understood. Once the door was wide open, Rafe stood aside and looked on as the mutt obediently loped past him, tongue dangling from the corner of his mouth.

After flipping on the lights and heat, Rafe called, "Come on, boy, let's get you some food."

Rafe watched, a bemused expression on his face as the dog lapped at the food, and wondered if he'd lost his mind by taking in the stray animal. The mutt had been at his back door several mornings ago, and he had fed him. Then he'd just disappeared and hadn't shown up again until now.

Crazy as it was, having the animal here seemed somehow to take the edge off his depression.

Once the dog had eaten and was curled up in the living room, Rafe headed for his bedroom and subsequently the bathroom. Minutes later he stepped out of the shower, dried off, and with the towel still draped around his waist, made his way into the kitchen. Opening the fridge, he got out a beer. Turning it up to his mouth, he drank half of it down without stopping.

Although he was hungry as well as thirsty, his stomach revolted at the thought of food. Maybe after he rested awhile he'd feel like eating, he told himself, grabbing another beer before sauntering down the hall to the living room.

After sinking into his easy chair and getting comfortable, he took another long pull on his beer. When he set the empty can on the floor, the dog's cold nose nudged his hand.

"I need to call you something," Rafe said, absently rubbing the top of the animal's head. "How 'bout just plain old Dog? That name all right with you?"

Dog thumped his tail in response.

Rafe laughed and laid his head back against the chair, hoping to feel his muscles unwind. But his body refused to cooperate, especially his gut. His insides were scraped raw. His thoughts were in total disarray. All because of a vision of loveliness that was Alison Young.

He should never have touched her. But in defense of himself, he hadn't been able to help it. Hell, how was he to know she'd go crazy over seeing a rat and nearly fall and hurt herself?

The mere memory of that moment when he'd held her tightly against him caused his stomach to knot and his sex to harden, both with a yearning he couldn't control nor understand.

Hell, he was a loner, always had been. Sure, there had been women, one night stands that had satisfied him physically, but never mentally.

Since prison, even those times had been few and far between. He had concentrated on nothing except getting his life back on track, turning it around, determined to make something of it. With that goal uppermost in his mind, he'd worked day and night to bring it about.

Returning to Monroe, however, had never figured into his plans. Here the memories were almost as painful as the ones from prison. But now that he was back, he was going to make the best of it. He was excited about the trees.

More than that, he was excited about Alison Young's sudden appearance in his life, brightening his stark, empty existence, even if it was only fleetingly. Still, she wasn't indifferent to him; he'd bet his last cent on that. In his arms, she'd been as hot for him as he'd been for her. He'd seen that heat in her eyes, felt it in her body.

So what was the deal? What lay behind that interest? Was she just a rich, bored widow out for a fling? He wished the hell he knew, but he didn't. What he did know was that for the first time ever, he wanted to become involved with a woman. Not just any woman, however, only Alison Young.

"Forget it, chump! While she might hire you, she's not about to crawl into your bed."

At the sound of his loud voice, Dog quirked an ear and whined again. Rafe dropped a hand and generously patted him on the head.

"Somehow I knew you'd understand, pal."

But did *he*? Did he understand that he could never have her? It was a fact of life that ex-cons simply don't fit with the rich and privileged.

Alison was certainly that. She was as cool and beautiful on the outside as an exquisite cut gem; yet underneath, he suspected she was smoldering and eager.

Touching her had been like catching a glimpse into paradise. She was perfection itself. One moment he'd been acting like a mere mortal, walking, talking, breathing, and the next, when she'd fallen against him, he'd ceased to exist on the conscious level.

Feeling the slope of her breast, feeling its pulsating softness against his hand had almost been his undoing. He'd imagined her nipple to be pink, like the insides of her lips, and hard. Thoughts of his mouth around that tiny bud heated his loins, made him weak with longing.

Groaning deeply, Rafe groped frantically for the other can of beer and popped the top. After taking a healthy gulp, he leaned back in his chair again, emotionally drained. His muscles were jerking in his legs, as if he had just run a marathon. He drank the last of the beer and closed his eyes.

He had come so close today to tasting the fullness of those honeyed lips, but he knew that wouldn't have been enough. He'd known then, and he knew now that he wouldn't be satisfied with anything less than tasting all of her.

As if sensing his pain, Dog lumbered up on his hind legs, laid his nose on Rafe's leg and moaned pitifully.

Rafe opened his eyes and looked down at him. "Yeah, I know, Dog, life's a bitch."

Nine

The next few days passed in rapid succession, despite the fact that Alison didn't work at the house on Maple Street. There were other pressing obligations that she had to attend to, such as a charity function she was in charge of and her volunteer work at the women's shelter.

Both were important, especially the time spent with the abused women and children. She had become interested in championing that cause shortly after Carter died, when a news article had pulled at her heartstrings. In the beginning she had shown her interest by donating money. Later she began spending time there as well, which she vowed to continue.

She also lunched with June and Heather, and spent an evening with Arthur. Of the three, the dinner with

Arthur was the least successful. While the evening had begun on a high note, it hadn't ended on one.

The minute they'd pulled out of the restaurant onto the street, he said, "Alison, I think it's time we talked."

She'd nodded, though she'd felt a stir of uneasiness.

"You know how I feel about you."

Alison glanced at his profile. His eyes were on the road as he drove with his usual caution, just as he did everything else. Impulsively, she laid a hand on his arm.

"You're nice," she said. "In fact, I think you're one of the nicest people I know, and I consider you a dear friend—"

"I'd hoped I could be more," Arthur interrupted quietly. "Friends, too, of course. But something more, much more. I want to marry you, Alison."

She swallowed against the lump that rose in the back of her throat. He was so good, so kind, and she hated to hurt him, but she had no choice.

"Oh, Arthur," she began, "I'm sorry, but—"

Again he interrupted her. "You can't." He paused with a sigh. "That's what you were going to say, wasn't it?"

"Yes," she said softly.

He was silent for a long moment, then taking his eyes off the road, he looked at her, a bittersweet expression on his face. "I can't say I'm not disappointed, because I am. But if you won't marry me, at least promise to continue to be my friend, let me be a part of your life."

Alison blinked back the tears. "I wouldn't have it any other way."

That conversation had taken place last evening, and now as she drove into the drive at the shop on a chilly but sunny afternoon, Alison felt nothing except relief. The matter with Arthur had been settled once and for all. However, that feeling of relief was short-lived when she looked next door and saw that the lot was empty. It was obvious Rafe had been working in her absence; the stands had been completed and the debris cleared away.

She sat down at her desk a few minutes later, after having fixed herself a cup of mocha. She was furious with herself for being disappointed that he wasn't there.

And while the incident with the rat had stirred revulsion, it had also stirred feelings she was unequipped to deal with.

It was foolish, however, to avoid him, especially since he was going to work for her. An objective person would tell her she hadn't used sound judgment in hiring him, a man about whom she knew almost nothing, and an ex-con to boot.

When she and June had had lunch, June had done just that.

"Tell me you didn't!" June all but shouted. "Tell me you didn't hire Rafe Beaumont."

Alison had glanced around the restaurant. "For heaven's sake, June, keep your voice down. And yes, I hired him."

"Have you lost your mind?" June berated her, leaning across the table, her red curls bouncing and her eyes sparking.

"No," Alison answered patiently.

"Then why on earth are you acting like you suddenly have some screws loose?"

Instead of taking offense, Alison laughed.

"It's not funny, Alison Young. Stop and think; the man's an ex-con. Why, he ... could rape you...."

"Oh come on, Juney," Alison said, "get real. He's not that kind of person."

"How do you know?"

"I just know," Alison said stubbornly, wishing she could explain her fascination with Rafe. But she couldn't because she didn't understand it herself.

"So you're going to do it your way, regardless?"

"That's right," Alison said firmly, but without malice.

June gave her a long, slow look. "I just hope you know what you're doing, my friend."

"Me, too," Alison responded. "Me, too."

Later, she had mulled over June's concerns, but in the end concluded a risk did not exist. She was proud of herself for taking the initiative, for making her own decision. If there were consequences, she'd just have to suffer them.

Pausing in her thoughts, Alison leaned back in her chair and sipped on the mocha, feeling its warmth penetrate her cold insides. All the while she listened for the sound of Rafe's truck, even when she knew she wouldn't be hearing it.

With that thought in place, she reached for her bag. Inside were containers and flowers. Since the majority of the paperwork was complete, she could now concentrate on creating her own designs.

She was so immersed in adjusting a flower so that it stood at exactly the right angle in an arrangement that she failed to identify the sound at first. It was only after the knock became louder that she realized that someone was pounding on the door.

"Coming," she called, laying down a silk rose and hurrying to the door.

Assuming it was one of her friends, she jerked it open. There stood Rafe.

"Sorry if I disturbed you," he said in his low, familiar voice, resting an arm against the door facing.

At the sight of him, Alison sucked in her breath.

Today was the first time she had seen him in anything other than his worn, earth-caked work clothes. He had on a beige chambray shirt and a pair of black jeans that fit his slim hips and muscled thighs to perfection.

The result was potent, making him look ruggedly attractive and more desirable than ever. With her limbs feeling suddenly boneless, she clung to the knob and forced herself to respond. "Would you like to come in? It's time I took a break."

"A break."

She smiled for real this time. "I've been hard at it, making arrangements."

"Oh, I see." He shifted his feet. "Well, I guess this wouldn't be a good time, then."

She frowned. "A good time for what?"

"To see my farm. The other day you said you'd like to see a Virginia pine."

She was startled, and it showed. "You mean now?"

His expression tightened, and Alison knew it wasn't so much what she'd said, but the way she'd said it that brought about that change in expression.

"Forget it," he said abruptly, backing away.

"No, wait . . . please." Alison's voice trembled ever so slightly.

He stopped in his tracks and waited.

"I didn't mean that the way it sounded. It's just that today. . . today isn't a good day. I'm sorry."

He made a gesture with his hand. "No apology necessary. It was a crazy idea anyway. I shouldn't have asked."

Turning, he walked down the steps.

"Rafe," she cried suddenly, hurrying out the door.

He twisted around, his gaze fixed on her in uneasy expectancy.

"I'll have to get my jacket and lock up."

"You mean you're coming?"

"Yes, and you knew I would."

Only he hadn't known. He hadn't known it at all. In fact, he'd expected her to tell him to go to hell.

Yet on the outside chance she would accept, he'd asked her. For days he'd abused himself, carrying around the picture of Alison on his bed, her arms outstretched to him. No music, no trimmings, just flesh—flesh that was warm and willing.

He knew he was crazy to pursue her. But those thoughts had unhinged him to such a degree that he'd been powerless to stop himself. And that was what scared him most of all.

Now, as he waited for her, shock augmented his fear. She was actually going with him; he couldn't believe it. What would they talk about, he wondered, once they got past the small talk?

Ah, what the hell, he thought, watching Alison as she bounded down the steps toward him, a tentative smile on her face. Who was he to look a gift horse in the mouth?

By the time she joined him at the edge of the sidewalk, she was out of breath. "Sorry, hope I didn't keep you waiting too long."

"Naw. We have plenty of time."

"Good," she said, this time giving him a real smile. "I couldn't decide if I was dressed appropriately or not."

Opening the door for her, he drawled, "You look fine."

Actually, she looked good enough to eat, he thought, taking in the white jacket that complimented a hot-pink jogging suit. The soft fabric emphasized the richness of her curves.

By the time he joined her in the close confines of the Blazer, his stomach felt like a gravel pit. It was only after he noticed her eyes on him that he reached in the pocket of his shirt and pulled out a piece of paper.

"Here are some figures I put together," he said in a matter-of-fact tone.

"Oh, good." Alison took the paper from him and lowered her long, dark, curling lashes.

While she studied the paper, he studied her, studied the way the sunlight highlighted her riot of blond curls. By itself, the color was extraordinary, but against the ivory fairness of her skin, it was dynamite.

He cursed inwardly just as she looked up from the paper. "Looks fine to me," she said softly.

"So you still want me to do the job?" he asked with forced calmness.

"Of course."

He shrugged. "Just making sure."

"When do you plan to bring the trees to the lot?" she asked, smoothly changing the subject.

"Thanksgiving Day, but starting tomorrow, Tom Lott, a friend of mine, and I will start cutting and delivering to nurseries, grocery stores and lots all over East Texas."

"Sounds like you've got your work cut out for you."

Rafe's mouth slanted into a smile. "That's an understatement, but I'm looking forward to it."

"How many acres do you have in all?" she asked, flicking a hair out of her face.

"Ten, but so far only four have trees planted on them." He paused and looked directly at her, laughter in his eyes. "And none, I promise, have any unsavory varmints lurking among them."

Alison chuckled and shook her head; when she did, his gaze locked on her throat, which was smooth and extremely delicate looking. Her chuckle was lighthearted and genteel, just as she was.

"I deserved that," she said huskily.

God, she was beautiful, he told himself, his heart stumbling. Again he questioned his sanity. What was he doing with this woman? She could have her pick of men, and he'd bet none would be a farmer with rough, calloused hands. And he'd sure as hell bet none would have been near a prison, much less in one.

At that moment Rafe realized he was about to miss his turn, and a terrible sense of hopelessness possessed him. He sighed and whipped the Blazer off the road, nosing it up a narrow lane.

"Are we here?" Alison asked.

"We're here," he said, his tone sharp, sharper than he intended.

He felt her eyes on him, but he stared straight ahead.

Ten

_____

Well, what's the verdict?''

For the past couple of hours Alison had trudged beside Rafe up and down the long rows, absorbing every word he'd said about the pines, relieved that his dark mood had passed the minute he'd parked in front of the house. Instead of going inside, they had gone immediately to where the trees were planted.

It was while they had wandered across the backyard, with the dog lapping at their footsteps, that Alison had taken in her surroundings. In the distance the wooded, sloping hills had caught her eyes. And from across a small meadow she could make out the top of a barn.

The second her feet had touched solid ground, not only had she felt a sense of peace and tranquility, but the beauty of the land had taken her breath away as well.

Now as she stood beside Rafe, that same feeling of awe was still with her.

"Well?"

His voice startled her out of her woolgathering. "I'm impressed, but then you knew I would be," she said, glancing up at him with a smile.

Rafe's face was serious. "No, I didn't, not really. Somehow I can't see you enjoying the outdoors."

"You're wrong," she said with feeling. "Even if I don't like to dig in the dirt, so to speak, I can still appreciate beauty when I see it."

"I guess that's what gets to me the most. It's so damn beautiful and peaceful. But, God, how I fought coming back."

He gazed off across the planted acres, his face wearing a brooding expression that suggested his thoughts were on another time, another place.

The wind had ruffled his dark hair, tangling it. Alison ached to reach up and touch it. But that, she knew, was out of the question.

"Aren't you glad you did?" Her voice was low and unsteady.

He looked down at her. "I've never thought about it one way or the other. I had to do what I had to do."

"Where did you work before you came back here?" she asked, realizing how little she knew about him.

"Houston," he said, seeming to take no offense at her question. "I worked for a large contractor, and not only did I hone my craft, I made damn good money as well."

"I think it's great when one enjoys his work."

He didn't miss the forlorn note in her voice. "And you don't enjoy what you do, I take it?"

"Not anymore."

"So too much of the good life is driving you to work, huh?"

Alison knew he was mocking her, but she refused to rise to the bait. "That's right. However, I do have a God-given talent for working with my hands." She paused with a smile. "Even though my sister isn't overjoyed about me opening the shop, she does concede that."

"She's special to you, isn't she?"

"How did you know?"

He shrugged. "The way your eyes lit up when you mentioned her."

"Actually, Heather's more like my daughter than my sister. She was a change-of-life baby. I was fifteen when she was born."

"Bet that was a shock," Rafe said, stuffing his hands in his pocket, causing the fabric to tighten across his thighs.

Alison looked away quickly, feeling the color surge into her cheeks. "It was, but it didn't take me long to come around, as she was such an adorable baby. Then, when my parents were run over and killed by a drunken driver, she came to live with me and Carter. She's always been a joy."

When he didn't comment, a silence ensued.

A few minutes later, he asked, "Have you seen enough?"

"If you're asking if I'm tired, the answer is no. I could walk for miles."

He gave her a lopsided smile. "That so?"

His smile, always in short supply but a treat when it came, caused her heart to turn over.

"That's so," she responded, not at all surprised by the huskiness in her voice.

"Well, since it's getting late, we'd best be moving on."

Again she trudged beside him, stopping only when he wanted to make a point, like now. He touched a pine needle.

"Don't you think these will look great with ornaments loaded on them?"

She laughed. "They'll be perfect."

"See, I was right about them being special, wasn't I?"

"Okay, so you're right. I am impressed," Alison said, meeting his gaze, basking under the warm insistence of it. She noticed a dozen other things at the same time—the ebony shine of his hair and the strength of his hands as he handled the foliage with tender, loving care. She knew he would handle a woman's body in exactly the same manner.

She averted her gaze and hurried ahead.

They walked in comfortable silence until they would have taken the worn path to the house, then Rafe said, "Let's take a detour. I want to show you something."

"What?" she asked, unable to sustain her curiosity.

"You'll see." His tone was as mysterious as it was noncommittal.

"Mmm, now you've really got me wondering."

"Good."

By the time they made their way beyond the barn and through a deep thicket, Alison's curiosity had gotten the best of her.

As if sensing that, Rafe said, "It won't be long now. It's just around the bend."

She peered up at him. "It?"

"Stop fishing," he said, his glance running warmly over her.

She laughed to disguise her breathless confusion. When he looked at her like that . . .

"How do you like it?"

She stopped, and directly in front of her was a log cabin. "Oh, Rafe, it's . . . it's beautiful."

"I'm kinda proud of it myself."

"Did you build it?"

"It's a kit, actually. I just put it together, only it's not complete. I still have to finish it."

Alison's eyes went wide with excitement. "Can I see inside?"

"Sure," he said, smiling. "That's why we're here."

"When did you find the time to work on it?" she asked, still shaking her head in amazement. They had toured the premises and were on their way back toward the farmhouse.

To say that she was impressed would be an understatement. Even unfinished, the log house was lovely. On the first level was a kitchen, den, bedroom, and bath, all with beamed ceilings. Upstairs was another

THE JOKER GOES WILD!

Play
this
card
right!

See
inside!

SILHOUETTE®
WANTS TO <u>GIVE</u> YOU

- 4 free books
- A free bracelet watch
- A free mystery gift

IT'S A WILD, WILD, WONDERFUL

FREE OFFER!

HERE'S WHAT YOU GET:

1. *Four New Silhouette Desire® Novels—FREE!* Everything comes up hearts and diamonds with four exciting romances—yours FREE from Silhouette Reader Service™. Each of these brand-new novels brings you the passion and tenderness of today's greatest love stories.

2. *A Practical and Elegant Bracelet Watch—FREE!* As a free gift simply to thank you for accepting four free books, we'll send you a stylish bracelet watch. This classic LCD quartz watch is a perfect expression of your style and good taste, and it's yours FREE as an added thanks for giving our Reader Service a try.

3. *An Exciting Mystery Bonus—FREE!* You'll go wild over this surprise gift. It is attractive as well as practical.

4. *Free Home Delivery!* Join Silhouette Reader Service™ and enjoy the convenience of previewing six new books every month, delivered to your home. Each book is yours for $2.24*—26 cents less than the cover price. And there is *no* extra charge for postage and handling! If you're not fully satisfied, you can cancel at any time, just by sending us a note or a shipping statement marked "cancel" or by returning any shipment to us at our cost. Great savings and total convenience are the name of the game at Silhouette!

5. *Free Newsletter!* It makes you feel like a partner to the world's most popular authors...tells about their upcoming books...even gives you their recipes!

6. *More Mystery Gifts Throughout the Year!* No Joke! Because home subscribers are our most valued readers, we'll be sending you additional free gifts from time to time with your monthly shipments—as a token of our appreciation!

GO WILD
WITH SILHOUETTE®TODAY—
JUST COMPLETE, DETACH AND
MAIL YOUR FREE-OFFER CARD!

*Terms and prices subject to change without notice. NY and Iowa residents subject to sales tax.

© 1989 HARLEQUIN ENTERPRISES LIMITED

GET YOUR GIFTS FROM SILHOUETTE®
ABSOLUTELY FREE!

Mail this card today!

PLAY THIS CARD RIGHT!

YES! Please send me my 4 Silhouette Desire® novels FREE along with my free Bracelet Watch and free mystery gift. I wish to receive all the benefits of the Silhouette Reader Service™ as explained on the opposite page.

(U-S-D-12/89) 225 CIS JAY3

NAME _____
                (PLEASE PRINT)

ADDRESS _____ APT. ____

CITY _____

STATE _____ ZIP CODE _____

Offer limited to one per household and not valid to current Silhouette Desire subscribers. All orders subject to approval.

SILHOUETTE BOOKS
"NO RISK" GUARANTEE

- There's no obligation to buy—and the free books remain yours to keep.
- You pay the low members-only price and receive books before they appear in stores.
- You may end your subscription anytime—just write and let us know or return any shipment to us at our cost.

IT'S NO JOKE!

MAIL THE POSTPAID CARD AND GET FREE GIFTS AND $10.00 WORTH OF SILHOUETTE NOVELS—FREE!

If offer card is missing, write to:
Silhouette Reader Service, P.O. Box 1867, Buffalo, NY 14269-1867

BUSINESS REPLY MAIL

FIRST CLASS   PERMIT NO. 717   BUFFALO, NY

POSTAGE WILL BE PAID BY ADDRESSEE

SILHOUETTE
READER SERVICE
901 FUHRMANN BLVD
PO BOX 1867
BUFFALO NY 14240-9952

NO POSTAGE
NECESSARY
IF MAILED
IN THE
UNITED STATES

bedroom in the form of a loft with numerous sky-lights above it and another bath.

"When you want to do something badly enough, you find the time," Rafe said. "However, if Tom and Gayle hadn't helped, I wouldn't be as far along as I am now. In no time, it'll be livable."

A few minutes later they reached the house. With a mocking glint in his eye, Rafe opened the door.

"Welcome to my humble abode," he said with a perfunctory wave of his hand.

Alison stopped just inside the door and looked around.

"It's in sad shape, I know," he added, standing close behind her, so close that she could feel his warm breath on her neck. "But it's home, and for now it meets my needs."

"Well, you know the old saying, 'There's no place like home.'"

There had been no apology in his voice for the run-down condition of the small house, and Alison had to admire him for that. Yet she felt a tight squeeze on her heart at the poverty still ingrained here, knowing that when he was growing up, it must have been twice as bad.

"Well, I won't deny I'm looking forward to living in the log house," Rafe added, his warm breath again caressing her neck.

She shivered, fighting the urge to lean against him.

"Sorry, I should've started a fire." Deserting her, he walked to the Franklin stove in the center of the room and knelt down.

Thank goodness he'd misunderstood her shiver, she thought, gazing around the room. There was a couch, a recliner, a rocker and a TV on a stand. The remainder of the furniture consisted of a scarred desk and a bookcase with books stacked in neat rows.

Beyond, she could see inside one of the two tiny bedrooms—there was a bed, neatly made, next to a chest of drawers. To her right was the kitchen.

In spite of its roughness and unadorned utility, the house was comfortable in a haphazard masculine way. It was a natural setting for him.

"Have a seat," Rafe invited without turning around.

She watched him poke at the log, as if under a tender spell.

When he got up and sat beside her on the couch, Alison shifted slightly in order not to touch him. For a moment they didn't say anything, content to stare into the fire and absorb its warmth.

"You want something to eat or drink?" he asked, reaching for her jacket that she was now discarding.

She shook her head, unknowingly causing her hair to swirl around her head like a silver cloud. "No, I'm fine."

His eyes narrowed, and he couldn't seem to pull his gaze away. "Ah, come on, what'd you say we have some hot chocolate?"

"Mmm, that does sound good. Want me to make it?"

"Nope," he said, getting up. "You stay put. I'll be back in a jiffy."

True to his word, he soon returned with two steaming hot mugs. He handed one to her, then sat down again.

"How do you plan to fix the log house up inside? Decorate it, I mean?" she asked conversationally, blowing on the dark liquid to cool it.

"Hadn't thought much about it, really. I've been too busy just trying to get the damn thing together." He shrugged. "Anyway, I'm not much on that sort of thing."

"Maybe I could help," she said sweetly.

"Does that 'maybe' mean you're volunteering?" he asked, looking at her over the rim of his cup.

Alison smiled. "Yeah, I guess it does."

He sat his cup down and took a mock swipe at his brow. "Whew! Thank God for small favors. No telling what it would look like inside if I had to decorate it."

"We won't even talk about that," she said teasingly. "However, you haven't done too badly with this place."

The humor left his face. "That's because there was only one way this place could go and that was up."

"Did you grow up here?"

"Yes." His eyes roamed the room. "And God, were we ever poor. I can remember times when we didn't have enough to eat."

"Is that what drove you to steal?" she asked softly, only to cringe inwardly when she watched his face turn gray.

"No," he said bitterly. "When I did that, my belly was full."

"Oh, Rafe," she whispered, "I shouldn't have said that. I...I know you don't like to talk about that time in your life. I'm...sorry if I hurt you."

The look he gave her caused her to tremble, and again the desire to touch him, to tell him that nothing was ever going to hurt him again was actually visceral. Tears glistened in her eyes.

"Aw, come on, it didn't hurt that bad." He paused. "Looking at you hurts worse."

"Oh, Rafe," she whispered again, the truth hitting her like a blow. This man had become far too important to her. He was confusing her, changing her—to such an extent that she no longer recognized herself. She had to call a halt before things got completely out of hand.

Uncertain as to whether the pounding of her pulse or the silence was the loudest, she stood suddenly. Wordlessly, he followed suit, his eyes never straying from her face.

The silence, like the shadows in the fire-lighted room, wrapped itself around them.

"Alison." His voice was as gravelly as coarse sandpaper.

"I...I should be going," she said when she could find hers.

"I want to see you again."

Though softly and evenly spoken, his words packed a wallop. Pretending to misunderstand, she said, "Of course, you'll see me again. You're going to work—"

"That's not what I meant."

Silence hung heavy as Rafe's eyes probed hers.

"Please...Rafe, take me home." Knowing that she was swaying unsteadily, Alison raised a hand to her breast in an involuntary motion.

With an agonized groan, he hauled her against him and tipping back her head, lowered his lips to hers. The passion she tasted instantly ignited the passion that was smoldering inside her. She strained against the hard length of his body and flung her arms around his neck. His lips were hungry, greedy—and rough, though his tongue mating with hers was warm and gentle.

She was trapped against him in shocking, aching need. Finally the pressure of his arms let up, and she wilted, taking deep, gulping breaths, telling herself again what madness it was to want him this way, to forget her priorities—forget everything.

She closed her eyes, but then she felt his lips again.

"Don't..." she gasped raggedly before his mouth found hers and stilled her cry. He plunged his hands through her hair roughly, possessively. Helpless, she clung to him.

Suddenly he pushed her away and stepped back.

"Come on," he said without emotion, "I'll take you home."

Eleven

―――

"Hey, sis, where's my red skirt?"

Alison paused and stared up at Heather, who was leaning on the balcony. "How should I know?" she said in loving exasperation. "I haven't worn it lately."

Heather's brows furrowed. "I'd believe that," she quipped.

"Exactly what is that supposed to mean?"

"You know what it means. Gee, sis, since you've been working on the shop, you've hardly worn anything decent at all. How long has it been since you've even had on a dress?"

"Yesterday, when I worked at the women's shelter."

Heather batted the air with her hand. "Ah, that doesn't count because I know you didn't get dressed up like you used to when you went to the club."

"That's right, I didn't, love." Alison flashed her sister an amused but patient smile. "And what's more, I'm not going to. Remember, I've turned over a new leaf."

Heather wrinkled her nose. "I'm not so sure I like the new you. What does Arthur think?"

"I wouldn't know."

"Now it's my turn to ask, 'What's that supposed to mean?'"

"It means that Arthur and I are just friends," Alison said. "And that's all we'll ever be." After seeing Heather's face fall, she smiled teasingly. "Hey, just because you're in love doesn't mean it's right for everyone else."

Heather answered her smile with a sheepish grin. "I guess so, but—"

"There's no 'buts' about it, at least not this morning. If you don't hurry, you're going to be late for your nine o'clock class."

A short time later Alison kissed Heather goodbye. When she turned and went back inside the big house, she felt a cloud of gloom settle on her.

She hadn't been at all surprised when Heather had arrived home yesterday afternoon to spend the night. Even though she loved the university and had a boyfriend, they had not replaced home.

But it wasn't Heather who was occupying her mind at the moment. It was Rafe. She hadn't seen or heard from him since that afternoon at the farm. She hadn't expected to, of course, she told herself hastily. Still...

Suddenly disgruntled with her thoughts, Alison went to the kitchen and paused at the coffeepot, where she filled a cup. Instead of wasting her time and energy on thoughts of Rafe Beaumont, she should be getting ready for Thanksgiving, which was only three days away. She had invited June and her husband, along with Heather's friend Tim.

But nothing short of a miracle could prevent her from thinking of Rafe and rehashing that dismal ride home from the farm.

They had made the trip home in virtual silence. She had sat like a statue and stared straight ahead, glancing at Rafe only when she couldn't help herself. It was obvious he'd been upset as well. His profile had looked like it was carved out of granite.

That was why she'd been so stunned when he'd walked her to the door and said, "I'll be in touch."

He hadn't gotten in touch, of course, which was for the best. She'd been right to put an end to their relationship. She must not see him again outside of a business environment. It would be both pointless and unfair because there could never be a satisfactory fulfillment. She was to blame for encouraging him in the first place. Her actions had provoked him into behaving exactly as he had.

Yet she'd had no idea that his kiss would unleash a flood of desire inside her so intense that she would be unable to shake it. Erotic dreams had haunted her, frightening her more than the loneliness that shared her bed each night.

She knew where his attraction lay. He was handsome. He was aloof. He was different. But most of all, he was wildly exciting. In his arms she'd been like a crazy woman, like a woman with an addiction. Which proved his danger. She wouldn't see him again. Period.

With this thought in mind, she picked up her coffee cup and made her way into the small workroom off her office.

She was halfway there when the phone rang. She answered it in her office.

"Hello."

"Am I interrupting anything?"

She recognized the rich timbre of his voice instantly; she almost dropped the receiver.

"No... I was just on the way to my workroom."

"Tom Lott, the friend I told you about, and his wife suggested I bring you to dinner. Thought you might like to take them up on the invitation."

She gripped the receiver tightly. Tell him. Tell him.

"I'd like that," she heard herself say instead, "that is—"

"I'll pick you up around six-thirty," he said, and hung up.

She didn't know how long she stood holding the receiver, staring at it.

"He's a different person when he's around you, you know?"

Alison stared at her hostess, who was standing beside her at the sink, a smile on her lovely face. Gayle Lott was tall and slender with slanted green eyes that many women would kill for and dark hair drawn back in a severe style that few women could wear. However, it wasn't her uncommon beauty that made her so special but rather her warm, generous personality.

The minute she had met Gayle and Tom, comical with his mustache and protruding belly, she had liked them, had felt instantly at home in their immaculate but modest home.

Alison returned Gayle's smile. "I was thinking the same thing only in relation to you and Tom, how relaxed and happy he is." Even as she spoke, ribald laughter drifted from the living room. "See, there. And I bet they're talking about us."

Gayle's eyes twinkled. "I wouldn't be surprised."

They had consumed a huge meal—roast and gravy, trimmed with carrots and potatoes, salad and blackberry cobbler. Afterward, while devouring a pot of coffee, they had played several games of forty-two. Now, the women were in the process of cleaning up while the men smoked and exchanged stories.

Gayle shook her head, her smile burgeoning. "Well, those two do go back a long way." She handed Alison another plate to dry. "Tom stood by Rafe during the trial and then afterward because he'd understood what made Rafe do the terrible things he did when no one else had." Her features, having darkened, suddenly brightened once again. "But that's all in Rafe's past, and he's well on his way toward building a new life for himself."

"He rarely mentions that time behind bars."

"We know very little ourselves," Gayle replied soberly. "We just know he suffered terribly."

"I know," Alison responded, feeling the prick of tears behind her eyelids.

They were quiet for a moment, as if they both needed time to regroup. Then Gayle said, "Back to my original statement, I've never known him to act this way around a woman."

"I'm sure there have been plenty of them," Alison said lightly, faking a smile.

Gayle shrugged. "A few. But as I said, he's never been so open, so carefree with any of the others. He kept his emotions completely in check." She paused and angled her eyes up at Alison. "But with you, when your eyes meet—wow! Even I can feel the sparks."

Alison's head snapped up. "That's your imagination."

Only it wasn't. Gayle was right. Every time her eyes and Rafe's met, which was often, the air around them seemed to quiver. Not once had he touched her, though he might as well have. She was aware of him with every nerve in her body, thinking how delicious he looked in dress jeans and a yellow sweater that played up his tanned skin.

Alison knew she looked her very best as well, having seen the warm glint in his eyes as they had wandered over her, taking in the simple purple knit dress that didn't quite reach her knees.

Suddenly realizing that Gayle was watching her with a strange smile on her face, Alison said staunchly,

"We're . . . we're merely friends, as in employer to employee."

Gayle's Chesire catlike smile deepened. "Sure, honey, and I'm going to be the next Queen of England, too."

"Hey, y'all gonna stay in here all night?"

Both women spun around. Rafe and Tom were standing just inside the kitchen door. Though Alison felt Rafe's eyes on her, she kept hers averted, Gayle's words having made more of an impact on her than she cared to admit.

With a chuckle, Gayle answered her husband. "We're just finishing up."

"How 'bout another game of forty-two, Alison?" Tom asked in a boisterous voice. "You up to it?"

This time she had no choice but to seek Rafe's eyes, a question in hers.

"I think we'll take a rain check," Rafe drawled, his gaze swinging to Tom. "It's getting late, and we have to move a load of trees in the morning, remember?"

Tom groaned. "How could I forget?"

Alison laughed; so did Gayle.

Minutes later Rafe climbed into the Blazer beside Alison, with Tom and Gayle standing on their steps, hands raised in farewell.

"Did you like them?" Rafe asked after they had rolled onto the highway.

"Very much," Alison replied warmly.

"I knew you would. They're special people."

"Mind if I ask you something?" Alison's tone was hesitant.

He faced her in the dark, an eyebrow arched. "Shoot."

"Were you and Tom laughing about me?"

"What?"

"Don't play dumb," she said. "You heard me."

"What makes you think that?"

She lifted her shoulders. "I don't know, just intuition, I guess."

"Intuition, huh?"

"Well, were you?"

His lips twitched. "As a matter of fact we were."

"Was it something you said?"

"Yeah, I told him you had a helluva cute butt."

"Rafe!"

He chuckled. "Is that all you've got to say?"

"No," she said primly.

He looked at her for a long moment, then laughed. In spite of herself, she joined in.

It was only after they pulled into the drive and Rafe shut off the motor that the mood suddenly changed. Even the silence that fell around them became taut.

Feeling Rafe's eyes on her, Alison folded her arms around her chest.

"You're cold. I'll turn the heat on."

"No, no. I'm all right."

The engine purred to life, and so did the heat. "You'll be warm shortly." Though he spoke quietly, his voice seemed to roar in the closed interior.

Once the warmth penetrated her bones, Alison unfolded her arms and placed a hand on the seat between them. His hand deserted the steering wheel and quickly covered hers.

The bottom dropped out of her stomach. She couldn't move, nor could she speak.

"Alison, look at me, please," Rafe coaxed thickly.

Unerringly, her eyes found his.

"Tell me what you want, what you really want."

What she wanted, that was a joke. When it came to men, to Rafe, she didn't know what she wanted. She put a hand to her breast. An ache began deep inside her. She was thirty-five and out of control, feeling like a small child alone in the dark.

"What...what I want is for us not to see each other again, not like this, anyway." When he would have interrupted, she went on, "It's for the best, for both of us."

He let go of her hand and swore violently.

Alison drew in a shuddering breath. She didn't blame him if he wanted to throttle her. There were names for women who strung men along, played with their emotions. Right now she didn't like herself very much. For a moment she looked out the window into the inky blackness, then wetting her lips, turned back to Rafe.

He was watching her. "I'm sorry, but that's the one thing I can't do."

"You have to," she said, her voice regaining its strength.

"Why?"

"For one thing, I'm too old for you. There's six years difference in our ages."

He scoffed. "So?"

"For another, our...our interests are different."

"Not that different."

"All right, our life-styles are different. You can't deny that."

"So? We can compromise."

"Oh, Rafe," she said, "you're deliberately making this difficult."

"You're damn right I am. Those are not valid reasons. They're cop-outs, and you know it."

"No, I don't know it," Alison said with conviction. "What I've said is the truth. Besides, there are other reasons."

"Spare me," he said, turning away, his lips twisted.

She placed a tentative hand on his arm and was shocked to feel the tenseness there. "Rafe...please."

He whipped around and in one swift move closed the distance between them, stopping only a hairsbreadth away. "For god's sake stop patronizing me! And give me credit for having a little sense. The real reason you don't want to see me is because I'm an ex-con, only you don't have guts enough to say it!"

For a second Alison was so flabbergasted by his accusation that she was speechless. Then she rallied, and cold, hard fury, equal to his, rose inside her.

"How dare you put words in my mouth when nothing could be further from the truth!"

"You're lying."

"I am not!" she cried, twisting and frantically searching for the door handle.

"Oh, no you don't," he said, and grabbed her and pinned her against the seat.

He swore again, only this time it was against her mouth.

Alison's frantic struggle died on a moan as his hand sought and found a pulsating breast. Her lips parted under his. The long, liquid kiss seemed to go on forever—mouth to mouth, tongue to tongue.

Suddenly, it was over. He released her and turned away, his profile dark and foreboding as the night around them.

Oh, God, she couldn't stand it, couldn't stand to see the pain and suffering on his face, knowing she was responsible. She had to make it go away. Somehow.

"Rafe," she sobbed, reaching out to him, touching him, "I didn't lie to you. You've got to believe me."

"Then prove it," he said so softly that at first she wasn't sure she heard him right.

"What . . . what did you say?"

"I said prove it."

Silence hung heavy.

"All right," she whispered, "I'll prove it."

He whipped around, his eyes glowing in the dark, but he didn't touch her. "Do you mean it?" His voice sounded hoarse, like he had a sore throat.

"Yes, I mean it," she whispered again. Why not? she defended herself. Why not continue to see him when that was what she wanted more than anything else in the world? Since Carter's death life had been empty; *she* had been empty.

The times with Rafe had changed all that. However, she was wise enough to know that they still had no future. They merely had one important thing in common: a quest to end their loneliness. For her, for now, that was enough.

"Hold me, Rafe," she pleaded achingly, "please hold me."

He needed no second invitation.

Twelve

Rafe's head was bathed in the sunlight spilling into the window of the Blazer. Watching him as he drove, Alison felt breathless, excited as she always did when she looked at him or got near him. He faced her suddenly, and their eyes met. For a moment everything seemed to stand still. Then reaching out, Rafe squeezed her hand before placing his own back around the steering wheel. Alison's heart pounded with oppressive force.

Instead of touching her hand, she wanted him to stop the vehicle and take her in his arms, kiss her again as he had this morning when he'd picked her up. She felt an aching hunger to be as physically close to him as it was possible to be. The calm happiness she had found in agreeing to see him had disappeared. Touching and kissing was no longer enough; she wanted more, much more.

For a week now she'd been with him constantly, except Thanksgiving Day, which he'd spent with his mother at the nursing home, while she'd followed through with her plans.

Yet Rafe hadn't made love to her. She knew why; he hadn't wanted to push her, or crowd her, knowing how unsure she'd been about their relationship. That considerate, caring attitude hadn't come as a surprise. Though he oftentimes acted like an embittered man with an ax to grind, he wasn't. Underneath that tissue paper macho was a gentle man who cared and seemed only to want to make her happy.

For herself it wasn't quite that simple. Still, she refused to dissect the reasons behind her decision, content to take one day at a time.

"What'cha thinking about?" Rafe asked in his warm drawl.

"How glad I am you let Tom mind the lot today so you could take me to market."

The day after Thanksgiving, Rafe's Christmas trees had officially gone on sale. Sales had been so brisk, he'd been extremely busy. But when he'd found out she was going to market in Dallas, he'd insisted on taking her.

"I wouldn't have missed it for anything."

"Pooh," she responded. "I know you were bored to death, especially with me walking up and down aisles and fingering practically every silk flower there."

Rafe chuckled. "I'll have to admit I thought you were going to end up buying the place out." He paused, the laughter in his eyes suddenly replaced by another emotion, a stronger one. "By the way, did I tell you how beautiful you looked?"

"No, no you didn't," Alison said, her voice faltering.

She had chosen to wear a Dior lightweight wool suit. Though it was simple in design, the color set it apart. The dark berry highlighted Alison's eyes and hair.

"You don't look so shabby yourself," she added when he remained quiet. He had on a pair of brown slacks and a tan sports coat.

"Well," he said, his lips twitching, "I couldn't go to the city looking like a country bumpkin, now could I?"

Alison tilted her head to one side. "You could never look like a country bumpkin if you tried. You're too gorgeous," she added seriously.

His lips twitched. "Think so, huh?"

"I know so," she said at last, the words a disjointed whisper.

His eyes darkened. "If you don't stop looking at me like that I'm going—"

"To what?" she challenged, turning her lethal smile on him.

"You'll see."

He no more than got the words out of his mouth before he whipped onto the shoulder of the highway. Luckily they were on a deserted stretch, because the second he jammed the car in park, he pivoted in the seat, reached for her and pulled her into his arms.

Rafe's lips were hot and demanding as they ground into hers. Finally pulling away for air, he trailed tiny kisses across her jawbone until he found her mouth again. Moaning, Alison looped her arms around his neck and strained against him, aching to feel every bone and every muscle in his body. They drank from each other's lips as if dying of thirst. His hand slid down and cupped one cheek of her buttocks, pressing her against his hardness while his kiss deepened.

Finally, he held her away from him slightly and said, "I couldn't keep my hands off you another second." His eyes burned into hers. "Not another second."

"I felt the same way," she whispered, watching while he undid the buttons at the neck of her blouse. Once that was done, he rubbed a thumb across a nipple, visible through the lacy bra, until it was hard and distended. It was impossible to determine whose breath was the most ragged when his lips sought hers yet again.

Suddenly a horn honked, followed by a wolf whistle and a shout. "Right on!"

They sprang apart as if they'd been shot and stared glassy-eyed at a teenager hanging out the window of a passing car.

Still stunned, they turned to each other and then burst out laughing.

When the laughter subsided, Rafe admitted ruefully, "This is the first time I've ever been caught necking in broad daylight."

Alison gave a shaky smile. "Me, too."

"Kinda enjoyed it myself. How 'bout you?"

She was capable only of shaking her head.

"Think you'd like to try it again soon?"

"Yes."

"Tonight?" The hunger in his voice was undeniable.

"Tonight," she echoed, feeling on fire.

Reluctantly, he dropped his hand, and they didn't say anything until they reached the city limits of Monroe.

"I need to check on Mother," Rafe said. "You wanna go with me?"

Alison didn't hesitate. "Yes, I'd like that."

He nodded and moments later parked the car in the nursing home parking lot. Holding hands, they made their way through the front entrance.

Rafe had just told her to wait there when Tom came striding down the hallway toward them, his face colorless.

Beside her Alison felt Rafe stiffen. "Tom, what the hell are you doing here?"

Tom halted in front of Rafe and placed an arm on his shoulder. "It's your mother—"

"She's dead, isn't she?" Rafe asked in a quiet, dull voice.

Tom sighed and gave Alison a quick glance before turning back to Rafe. "Yes, I'm sorry to say, she is."

Alison wasn't sure she was doing the right thing by intruding on Rafe's grief, but she couldn't help herself. Even now, turning into the road that led to the farm, she had to force herself to slow down or risk tearing something loose under her car due to the ruts in the road. It had rained the entire day, and with dusk approaching, it was threatening again.

Two days ago Rafe had buried his mother, and she hadn't seen him since. Tom had continued to substitute for him at the lot.

It had drizzled throughout the sad service, and Rafe had stood stoically beside Tom and Gayle without so much as a coat on.

Alison had ached to go to Rafe and put her arms around him, hold him, comfort him. But she hadn't. From the moment Tom had told him about his mother, he'd shut her out. He'd become an unapproachable stranger. It was as if his mother's death had opened old wounds that he was having difficulty dealing with.

But enough was enough. She wouldn't be shut out any longer. She had made the commitment to be a part of his life, and she was damn well going to see it through. Besides, she missed him, missed him terribly.

When she got out of the car a few minutes later, there were no lights on. But she knew he was home. Both the pickup and the Blazer were parked to the side.

Refusing to acknowledge the sinking feeling in the pit of her stomach, Alison walked to the door and knocked. No answer. She knocked again. Still no answer.

Boldly she opened the door and peered around it. "Rafe."

It wasn't until he moved out of the shadows and into the light that she saw him. Her heart turned over at his appearance. A dark stubble emphasized the harsh lines creasing his face. For once he looked older than his years, dressed in old jeans and a shirt that was completely unbuttoned. His hair was mussed as if he'd continually plowed through it.

"May I come in?" she asked softly.

His eyes were tormented. "Dammit, Alison, you shouldn't have come."

"Why?" she whispered, closing the door behind her. A fire was crackling in the Franklin stove, giving the room a cozy warmth that was welcome to Alison's chilled heart.

"When I'm like this, I'm no good to myself or anyone else."

She flinched against his ruthless tone, but walked toward him nevertheless. "I know you're upset because your mother died, and well you should be, but—"

"You want to know why?" he asked harshly. "Well, I'll tell you. It's because it's such a waste." He paused and stared at her in the dim light. "Ah, what the hell, you wouldn't understand—"

"Please, don't shut me out," she pleaded. "Help me to understand."

He sighed, and for a moment Alison thought he wasn't going to answer, but then he said bleakly, "There's so much you don't know about my life."

"Tell me," she encouraged softly.

His eyes hardened. "When Mother died, it brought back the bitterness against my father, a bitterness that makes me crazy, even violent at times. I feel now exactly the way I felt when I stole those cars. And that scares the hell out of me. Everything was falling apart inside me and I was . . ."

"Desperate," Alison finished for him, tears gathering in her eyes.

"How'd you know?"

"I've been there, too, only the circumstances were different."

His features contorted. "I don't think so, Alison. Your father didn't bring disgrace on your family every waking moment of every day."

"No, he didn't," she responded gently.

"Well, mine did."

"Was it because your dad didn't work?" she prodded gently.

"That's rich." A bitter laugh escaped his lips. "He stayed too drunk to work."

"What did he do, if he didn't work?" she asked innocently, totally unprepared for his answer.

"Beat on my mother, mostly. When I came home from school, he'd start on me. I tried to please him, but no matter what I did or said, it was wrong. The more I said, the more he knocked me around."

"Oh, God," Alison whispered, her stomach revolting.

She'd known there were carefully bricked-up emotions in him that he rarely let surface. She'd seen the anger. On rare occasions true laughter had surfaced. But never had she seen the pain, the deep-seated pain that was revealed in his eyes at this very moment.

What price had he paid, she wondered, for keeping it locked inside?

Knowing he didn't want or expect her pity, she swallowed the lump in her throat and asked quietly, "Why didn't your mother take you and leave?"

He shrugged. "Who knows? Maybe fear that she couldn't make it alone. She had no skills. Or maybe she was afraid he'd kill us."

"Did he ever stop drinking?"

"Yeah, otherwise he couldn't have planted the trees. Only his sobriety came too late as far as Mother was concerned. She'd already had one massive stroke and several light ones."

"Leaving her a vegetable."

"And I can't help but blame myself!" His bitter cry came straight from the heart. "If only I hadn't gotten into trouble and been around, I might have done something to help."

He stopped and seemed to struggle for his next breath. "God help me, I didn't even have a chance to tell her I was sorry."

He turned away, but not before Alison saw the tears in his eyes. "Oh, Rafe," she said achingly, her own tears falling unchecked. She was aware of nothing but him, his nearness, his pain.

It was then that she knew she loved him, loved him with all her heart. The full ramifications of that love wouldn't hit her until later, she was sure, but for the moment just admitting it was enough.

"Go back where you came from, Alison," he said, turning his back and walked to the window. "Forget me. Go back to your safe, secure world. I'm used to being alone."

It was inconceivable to her that he was so near, and yet she was forbidden to hold him, to console him, to love him. Anything less than that was unnatural and abhorrent.

"You're not alone," she said unsteadily. "You have me."

"No I don't. Not really." He sounded weary, far away, as though he were speaking from behind a barrier of brittle glass.

Now was the time to tell him she loved him, to shatter that barrier, but for some reason the words wouldn't come. It was as if a giant hand squeezing her throat refused to let her speak.

"Rafe, why, why are you doing this?" she cried. "Please..." Her voice caught on a sob. "Please just don't send me away." Love had suddenly become a disease, hurtful and cruel.

His hesitation was only minuscule. In one quick move he whirled around, grabbed her and folded her against him. "Oh, God, Alison, don't cry," he begged. "Please don't cry. I don't want to hurt you— you of all people," he whispered against her lips.

"Hold me, Rafe," she said. "Make love to me."

"You mean it?" His eyes glistened.

"Oh, yes."

Together they made their way into his bedroom. Evening shadows stole around the room. Yet there was no chill in the air. The fire from the stove, combined with the heat radiating from their bodies, kept them warm as they shed their clothing.

When Alison stood before Rafe in naked splendor, his eyes moved slowly over her, devouring every delectable inch of her body, the high, rose-tipped breasts, the flat planes of her stomach, the hidden shadows at her thighs.

"Oh, Alison, you're perfect." His voice shook with passion.

"I'm glad you think so," she whispered, feeling her flesh tremble as he pulled her to him again, and they sank onto the bed.

Silently, he touched his lips to the softness at her neck, his tongue tasting the slightly salty moisture he found there. She quivered at the fiery lick the caress ignited in her.

"Soft, so soft," he murmured, concentrating now on her breasts where he nuzzled first one, then the other. With a moan Alison's arms enveloped him, her fingertips sliding up and down his back, encouraging him. Her trembling thighs expressed her delight.

His hands praised her eagerly; his tongue laved her gently. It seemed to her that she was filled with an unbearable heat, as if she were trapped in a furnace. Her legs parted so that when he eased down, the stubble of his beard rasped the tender flesh on the insides of her thighs. She shivered and whimpered over and over while his lips and tongue robbed her of all coherent thoughts.

When her eyes finally fluttered open, Rafe was staring down at her, his eyes shining.

"I'm aching," he whispered. "Here. For you." He took her hand and placed it on hardness.

The instant her fingers surrounded him, her heart slammed against her chest. She felt him expand, and for a long, flawless moment she dared not move, content just to hold him. It was perfect, electrifying because of the feeling, stimulating because of the anticipation.

"I want to be inside you," he rasped. "Is that what you want?"

"Yes . . . please!"

Unable to contain himself a second longer, he shifted onto the full length of her body. Her legs spread of their own accord. She brought his mouth down to her breasts the instant he thrust inside her.

Basking in his deep-seated moan as his lips surrounded a sensitive nipple, she dug her nails into him and felt him spill deep into her. With a small cry she joined him in exquisite release.

Thirteen

An unutterably incredible sensation woke him.

When Rafe opened his eyes, it was still dark, but not dark enough that he couldn't see Alison nestled in the crook of his arm. An intense pleasure seized him.

Careful not to disturb her, he turned his head toward the clock on the bedside table. Twelve o'clock, and he was wide awake. He wanted a cigarette badly, but he wouldn't indulge, knowing that any movement on his part would awaken Alison.

Sighing inwardly, he once again stared at the sleeping figure beside him, content for the moment to do only that. He considered it a miracle that she was here in his arms. Most of his life had been a series of regrets, from his childhood through his adult years. No longer. Alison made the difference. She was the best thing that had ever happened to him.

In the beginning he'd denied the feeling that churned inside, identifying it as nothing more than hot, scalding desire, likening Alison to a delicious piece of fruit, tempting but forbidden. She'd represented the kind of woman he'd always wanted but knew he could never have.

Now he knew it wasn't just desire that had lured him to her, it was love. Foolhardy as it might be, for the first time in his life he had fallen in love.

She's mine, he found himself thinking, the thought nearly knocking the top of his head off. *Mine.* He tested the words silently on his tongue. It seemed right, exhilaratingly right.

But she wasn't his and never would be. And now that he'd found her, how could he let her go?

His eyes rested on the top of her head, the silver strands of her hair tickling his chin and chest. One of her slender legs was draped over his, the tip of her knee touching his manhood.

Their lovemaking had been perfect. There had been times when he hadn't had to move at all, her quivering response was so articulate. She had surrounded him like a scented cloud, and he'd felt suspended in time and space.

"Rafe," she whispered against his side.

His hold tightened. "Mmm?"

"Are you awake?"

He smiled in the dark. "Sort of."

"What time is it?"

"Our time," he said tenderly.

She answered with a touch instead of words. Shifting so that her head was cradled in the palm of her hand, she ran the soft tip of one finger down the ugly scar on his side.

Slowly, under her tender ministrations, Rafe felt his insides melt.

"Does it hurt?" she whispered, gazing up at him.

"No, no it doesn't hurt." He sucked in a short, involuntary breath. "At least not the scar itself."

"But you hurt on the inside when you think about it, don't you?"

He placed his fingers on her hand and stilled it. "Yes," he sighed.

"You never told me what happened," she said softly.

"Oh, Alison, you don't want to know the details. They're so sordid, so ugly. Those years were the worst in my life, and up till then there were some bad ones, believe me."

"Did . . . did you almost die?"

"Yes," he answered reluctantly. "I was trying to defend a young boy who had offended one of the prison's gang members."

"Go on," she urged.

"To keep his cronies from bashing the kid's head in, I interfered. You know the rest." Feeling her muscles tighten, he added, "I told you it wasn't a pretty story."

"Those places must be as bad as they say," she replied, her voice cracking.

"It's worse," Rafe said, staring into space. "Prison is a stinking hellhole and I'd die before I went back." God, he hated to even think about that time in his life, much less talk about it. But he knew he must. He wanted there to be no secrets between them. "And when I got out, it was almost worse. I was like a fish out of water."

Silently, she reached up and touched him. He looked down into her eyes and saw that tears were streaming down her cheeks. Shocked, it dawned on him those tears were for him. He ached to trap each one in his hands; to him they were more precious than gold.

"Oh, Alison," he said, "you're the best thing that's ever happened to me. You heal me."

She lifted her head and kissed him on the lips; he tasted her salty tears as he drew her close to his heart. The breath that passed between them was as warm as love.

Alison awakened to a weak sun trying its best to get through the blinds and make itself known. A second sense told her that Rafe was still asleep. Loosening herself from his hold, she twisted and faced him. His eyes were closed, his lashes lying long and thick against his cheek. He looked so relaxed, so young, she thought with a pang. She turned away and blinked back the tears.

Suddenly she felt him move. Turning back around, she saw that his eyes were open. There was a possessive look in them.

"How long have you been awake?" she asked.

"Long enough to make sure I didn't dream you."

Seeing him stare at her with that vulnerable look in his eyes was heart-wrenching. He raised his hand then, and laid the back of it against her cheek. The tender caress reminded her of his strength—and his gentleness. "Rafe—"

"I love you, Alison."

"And I love you," she said without hesitation.

His jaw went slack, and his eyes narrowed. "Are you sure?"

"I'm sure."

"Then marry me."

"Marry you?" she repeated, dumbfounded.

"In the evenings after I finish at your shop, I can work on the log house. It'll be ready in no time."

Her confused emotions rendered her speechless. She shouldn't have been surprised. Wasn't that just like him—a man of action, not of words? And where she was concerned, his motives were clear and simple. He wanted her and that was that.

"I want to marry you," he stressed, "even though I know I'm not good enough for you—"

"Oh, Rafe, don't say such a thing. Don't even think such a thing. You're a good man, only—"

"Only what?"

He watched her steadily. His face didn't show it, but Alison knew that he was as deeply shaken by their confessions as she was.

"I'm not sure . . . about marriage," she faltered.

"If not marriage, what? An affair?" His voice had turned hard, his mouth grim.

"Of course not," she said, feeling a flush stain her cheeks. Why did he have to cloud the heady moment by pressing her for an answer? For the moment she only wanted to savor the knowledge that he loved her.

She didn't want to make a decision about marriage. She didn't want to make a decision about anything.

"I love you, Alison. I don't want to lose you."

"There's no chance of that," she said, her mouth etched in a beautiful smile.

"Are you sure?" He didn't sound convinced.

"Yes, my love. We have time. All the time in the world."

"Do we? When I was in prison, I sensed death around every corner. Since then, time to waste is something I don't have. That stink hole swallowed a chunk of my life. I want to make the rest of it count—with you."

Alison traced the outline of his lips, deeply grieved by the sadness in his life, for the things that had been taken away from him. She wanted to say that she'd marry him; she yearned to say it. But she couldn't.

"I love you, Rafe," she said instead, "with everything that's in me. Why can't that be enough for now?"

"Because I want it all."

His quietly spoken words shook her. She turned ashen.

"Are you saying that if I don't marry you, you . . . you won't see me anymore?"

"What would be the point?" he demanded sharply, almost angrily. "If you love me, you'll marry me. Now."

She opened her mouth to speak, then closed it suddenly, realizing she had no suitable comeback. All she could do was stare at him wide-eyed.

"As it is, when I don't see you I'm so damned miserable I'm not worth killing. You're on my mind twenty-four hours a day. I'm nearly crazy. That's why I'm willing to break my back finishing the log house, so we'll have a place that's ours to live. That's why I want to marry you."

"Oh, Rafe," she whispered gently, gazing at his face drawn with indignant anger, "can't you see that marriage between us won't work? Even if we forget the age difference, there are still other problems. I've been married, and I have a sister who is my responsibility."

"I know all that."

"Then you should find you a nice girl your age or younger to marry."

"I don't want a girl," he said savagely. "I want a woman. I want you."

Determined to make him understand, Alison added ruthlessly, "You'll be cheating yourself—because I can never have children." There, she'd said it; she'd delivered what was certain to be the severing blow.

He didn't so much as flinch. "So what? I don't want children. I want you, only you."

"You say that now," she said in a strained voice, "but later you'll wish you had a child, a son perhaps. Carter never forgave me because I couldn't give him one. And I never forgave myself. I always felt like a failure." A tiny shiver shook her body. "I can't . . . I won't go through that again. Maybe if you were older, had children of your own, it might work. But since you don't, marriage between us is out of the question."

He grabbed her suddenly, as if the thread that held his temper had snapped, and kissed her. His mouth was rigid and inflicted pain. Then pushing her to arm's length, he stared down into her eyes.

"Tell me, is that out of the question as well?"

"You know it isn't," she cried, sagging against him, conscious of the hard, packed muscles against her.

"Then dammit, stop looking for excuses. If you love me, we can make it work."

Was it possible? Suddenly his words made sense. Of course it was. There was no other way. In order to possess him, she had to marry him. He was right, their love was worth more than a casual affair, to even think otherwise only cheapened it.

She knew that; she knew herself. She knew she was incapable of less than a complete commitment to love. Denying it, she had merely deceived herself. Loving him under any other conditions would be unacceptable.

Yet she knew there would be troubled times ahead. Marrying Rafe would not be easy. There were a multitude of problems to deal with. But more than anything, there was Heather. Later she would think of her sister, and her friends. But not now.

"Alison?" The word came out sounding like a groan.

She smiled through her tears. "I'll marry you. I can't imagine not marrying you. I should have known it all along."

"As long as you know it now, my darling, that's what counts," he whispered, casually thumbing a nipple.

"It won't be easy. You'll have to give me time, time to adjust."

"But not too long," Rafe added, concentrating on the other nipple.

"You'll...you'll help me?" she asked, seeking further reassurance despite the scalding ache between her legs.

He answered her by shifting slightly, then entering her with an urgency that made her gasp with pleasure.

"Is this what you had in mind?" he said, his voice strangled with desire.

"Perfect," she said. "Just perfect."

Fourteen

——

Two hours later Alison maneuvered her car in and out of the late morning traffic as if in a daze. Twice she had to be honked at to move through a green light. Her thoughts were filled with Rafe and the commitment she had made to him. Both excitement and apprehension had a stranglehold on her, the latter being the stronger of the two.

When they'd finally gotten out of bed, Rafe had prepared breakfast, and much to his amusement she had eaten like a starving woman.

"You're a better cook than I am," she'd told him, grinning. "I can't eat at this rate much or I'll get fat."

"Where?" he said, returning her grin.

"That," she countered saucily, "is my business." Then after a moment's thought she asked, "Do you like the way I look?'' A wave of color flooded her face. "I mean..."

He hesitated on purpose; she was sure of it. His eyes twinkled. "Well, now, let me see..."

"Stop teasing and tell me. I want to know."

"When you came over and introduced yourself that day, I thought you were the most beautiful creature I'd ever seen," he said. "And I still do."

A soft sigh split her lips. "What a lovely thing to say."

"It's the truth."

"Did you feel anything besides anger?" she asked shyly.

"Something I've never felt before, though I'm not sure I can explain it. An eager anticipation, maybe," he said, then frowned. "This sounds corny as hell. But you seemed to walk on air like an angel, and even though I gave you a hard time, I knew you were as nice as you were beautiful."

Her throat choked with sudden emotion. "That's a wonderful thing to say," she finally whispered.

In between tender looks and touches, they tidied the house. It was only after she was dressed and ready to go that she felt the first ripples of uneasiness.

"There are so many things I have to take care of," she reminded him. "It has suddenly hit me just how many. First thing is Heather. I'll have to tell her. And then there's the house. I'll have to do something about it."

Silently she resented the practical problems that were now intruding on her happiness.

"Hey, take it easy. You're supposed to look forward to getting married, not dread it."

"I'll have to have time," she stressed to make sure he understood.

He kissed her feverishly, passionately, wetly. She clung to him, her knees buckling.

"But not too much," he pleaded huskily. "I'm not a patient man."

Now, as she turned into her driveway, Alison looked at the house that had been her home for so long with renewed interest. A frown marred her features. How could she leave it?

Without warning, guilt stabbed her. Guilt for what? For whom? Carter? Was she feeling guilty because she hadn't loved him with the same reckless intensity that she loved Rafe?

Furious with herself, she bolted out of the car. Her forehead drawn in a faint frown, she fitted the key into the familiar lock. In the hallway a chill swept over her. Instinctively, she knew something was wrong.

She stepped cautiously down into the sunken living room and froze. "Oh, no!"

Directly in her line of vision was a huge painting. Behind that painting, the wall housed a safe. The painting, however, was no longer in place. It was on the floor, and the safe was gaping open. Empty. All her jewelry, with the exception of what she kept in her bedroom, was gone.

"Oh, no," she whimpered again, her eyes sweeping the room. Nothing else seemed to have been tampered with, she thought wildly. Though it was an effort, she forced her rubbery legs to move and tore up the stairs to her bedroom, the jewelry box uppermost in her mind.

The moment she crossed the threshold, she paused. "Damn, damn, damn."

The room had been ransacked. Drawers were open, items strewn everywhere, her jewelry box rifled. On closer observation, there was not one piece of jewelry left, not even the costume pieces.

Lowering herself onto the side of the bed, Alison struggled for air. It wasn't her jewelry being gone she found so abhorrent, although that was bad enough, it was the idea that someone had invaded her home, pilfered her belongings. She folded her arms across her chest, while a creepy feeling slithered over her skin.

Several moments passed before she got her bearings. Her first thought was to call Rafe. She needed his stability, needed his arms around her. Then she remembered he'd planned to leave town to deliver trees.

Fighting back the tears, Alison breathed deeply, then stood and crossed to the telephone where she dialed the police station.

"This is Alison Young on Echo Lane. I'd . . . like to report a burglary. . . ."

"Are you sure you don't want me to come over?" Rafe asked again, his voice pitched low with concern.

"No, I'm fine now, really I am."

And she was. Just hearing Rafe's voice, even if it was over the phone, perked her up, put things in their right perspective.

She had awakened only seconds ago and before she did anything else, she'd called him. When she'd told him what had happened, his sharp expletive had brought a smile to her lips.

"Alison, why didn't you call last night?" he asked, his tone a reprimand. "You shouldn't have stayed there alone."

"I know, but I made it all right. After the police left, I put things back in their place, went to the shop and worked the rest of the day. Afterward, I came home, showered, took two aspirins and fell into bed."

"What did the police say?" Rafe asked.

She sighed. "Apparently there's been a rash of burglaries in this neighborhood. Some houses have been hit in broad daylight, which is what happened here, the police think."

"Will I see you today? Tonight?"

A warm feeling rushed through her at the wary eagerness in his voice. "Yes, to both," she whispered.

A short time later, over coffee, her heart raced once again when she recalled Rafe's muttered, "I love you," just as he hung up. Those words didn't come easy to him, she knew. And that was why they meant so much to her.

Smiling, she got up and reached for the coffeepot. It was then that she heard two car doors slam simultaneously. Rushing to the window that allowed her access to the drive, Alison saw Heather get out of one car and June another.

"Well, isn't this a nice surprise," Alison exclaimed, opening the door and hugging Heather first, then June.

Heather dumped her purse and bag onto the nearest chair and headed for the pantry. Opening it, she grabbed a box containing Little Debbie Cakes. "The faculty's having some kind of meeting this afternoon, so we all got walks in our classes," she said, taking a cake out and removing the wrapper.

"I decided to come home since Tim is working on a project and can't be disturbed." She grinned at Alison. "Thought we might do a little shopping if you can tear yourself away from Maple Street long enough."

"Now that, dear girl, sounds like a great idea," June chimed in enthusiastically, winking at Alison while helping herself to a cup of coffee. "Mind if I tag along?"

"We'd love it. Right, sis?"

Alison shook her head. "Hey, you two, slow down. Have you forgotten I have work to do?"

Heather made a face. "Just listen to her, Juney. If she's this gung ho now, think of what we'll have to put up with later."

"I'd rather not," June said with a teasing shudder.

Alison, squelching the urge to throttle them both, smiled with saccharine sweetness instead. "Just wait until Silk Reflections becomes the talk of the town. You'll be sorry you made fun."

"By the way," June asked, her face suddenly serious, "how are things progressing?"

"All right," Alison began, only to be interrupted by the doorbell.

Heather gulped down the last of the cake. "I'll get it," she said, scurrying toward the door.

"You've done a great job with her," June said, watching Heather disappear. "You ought to be proud of yourself."

"I am, believe me." Alison's smile bordered on sadness. "She's the child I never had."

Heather chose that moment to return, a frown on her face.

"What's wrong?" Alison asked, alarmed.

"It's a policeman, sis. He wants to talk to you."

Alison sighed. "I'm not surprised. We . . . were broken into," she said, her eyes on Heather. "I just hadn't gotten around to telling you."

"You mean someone broke in here!"

"Shh, keep your voice down," Alison said sharply, then felt bad. After all, Heather wasn't the one at fault; she was. She shouldn't have blurted out the fact that they had been robbed. But then she hadn't expected the police back so soon either. "They took my jewelry, nothing more," she added in a gentler tone.

"Oh, dear, what a pity," June said, holding her hand over her heart. "All those gorgeous rings . . ."

"We'd best not keep the officer waiting," Alison said, and turned her back on them, assuming they would follow.

Once they were in the living room and the polite introductions out of the way, Officer Jackson came straight to the point.

"I thought you might like to know we have a lead, Ms. Young. The neighbor across the street, a Mrs. Willard, said she remembered seeing a tall, dark-headed man wandering around the neighborhood this past week."

Alison's face brightened. "That's certainly good news, Officer."

"Do you by any chance know a Rafe Beaumont?"

Alison flinched visibly, as if she'd been dealt a blow to the stomach. Her face turned deathly white. Suddenly, every eye in the room was on her. "Yes...I know him. But—"

"Oh, my God," June rasped, as if she, too, sensed what was coming.

Officer Jackson turned to her. "Do you know him, ma'am?"

"Well...er...I...I..." June began, clearly flustered, "not really, Officer. I just know the name and that...that he's selling Christmas trees on the lot next to Al...Ms. Young's rent house," she finished lamely.

"Why are you asking about Rafe Beaumont?" Alison asked in a cold voice.

"Well, ma'am, based on what Mrs. Willard said, we questioned him this morning in connection with the thefts."

Alison gasped aloud this time, and for a second she thought she might faint.

"Sis, are you all right?" Heather cried.

"Alison!" June's voice matched Heather's in hysteria.

Alison opened her mouth, but no words came out. She licked her lower lip, feeling as if she were on stage, in a play, suddenly unable to remember her lines.

She had to say something, but what? The truth. No! Not like this. Oh, God, she didn't want Heather to find out about her and Rafe like this. But what choice did she have? She had to tell the truth.

"Ms. Young?" Officer Jackson prodded.

"You needn't question Rafe Beaumont any longer."

"Why is that, ma'am?"

Alison raised her chin. "Because Rafe Beaumont was with me. All night."

This time the gasps came from Heather and June. They stared at Alison in horror while Officer Jackson looked down at his brightly polished shoes.

Finally, when the silence reached a screaming pitch, the officer cleared his throat. "If you'll excuse me, ma'am, I'll be going. I'll be in touch later."

With a nod to the others, he pivoted on his heels and walked out, leaving behind a stark, hostile silence.

Heather was the first to recover. "What's going on, Sis? I...don't understand. Who is Rafe Beaumont?"

"He's a carpenter and a farmer," June put in, a disapproving slant to her lips. "And an ex-con."

Heather blinked, then fell back onto the couch as if her legs had suddenly given out on her. "Ex-con?" she wheezed.

"June, please," Alison bit out furiously. Then focusing her attention back to Heather, she added, "There's so much you don't understand. I know I should have told you that I'd been seeing someone, but it all happened so suddenly..."

Heather's eyes were coldly accusing now. "What did you mean when you said you'd been with him all night? Does that mean you slept with him? Slept with a man who's been in prison?"

Again Alison flinched. The way Heather said it made what she and Rafe had shared seem sleazy, dirty. And while she wouldn't tolerate their love being smeared, it was imperative she use patience in dealing with her sister. After all, this had come as a brutal shock.

"Yes, Heather," she explained, "I slept with him because I'm in love with him." When Heather would have interrupted, she held up her hand. "No, let me finish. And yes, he's been in prison, but that's behind him. He's recently come back to Monroe, to the family farm where he's growing Christmas trees. In between he works as a carpenter. He's doing the work on the shop."

Pausing, Alison crossed the room and knelt in front of Heather, a pleading glint in her eyes. "Oh, honey, he's a fine, caring man. When you meet him, you'll see that."

"I don't want to meet him."

"You don't mean that," Alison responded gently.

"Yes, I do," Heather cried, and lurched off the couch, her curls bouncing around her flushed face.

Alison stood, aching to put her arms around her sister and hold her. She knew what was wrong; Heather was jealous.

Heather's eyes left Alison's and sought June's. "Did you know about...about him, Juney?"

June glanced at Alison. "No...no I didn't."

"How could you do this to me?" Heather whimpered, recoiling from Alison.

Alison wasn't above pleading. "I can understand how you feel because I'm still a little stunned by it all myself. I'm just sorry you had to find out like this. But in time you'll adjust."

Heather laughed harshly. "I'll never adjust. It's...it's absolutely insane, that's what it is." Her humorless laughter had turned to tears; they were coursing down her cheeks. "I can imagine what Tim will think. And his family. And other people. Oh, God—" Her voice caught on a sob.

Alison went toward Heather again, her heart feeling like a chunk of lead in her chest. "Please, honey—"

"How could you do this to me?" Heather shouted.

Before Alison could reply, Heather turned and ran from the room.

"Oh, Alison, what have you gone and gotten yourself into now?" June asked, shaking her head, tears swimming in her eyes.

Alison didn't say anything. Instead, she wilted onto the couch, stunned, as if she had suddenly run into a wall while walking in the dark.

Fifteen

By the time Alison arrived at the shop, she was a bundle of nerves.

She had planned on getting there much earlier in the day; she'd been worried about Rafe, worried about his frame of mind after the police had questioned him. Her plans hadn't worked out, however. Most of the day had been taken up with Heather.

The moment June had left, she had gone to Heather's room and knocked. Though a muffled "go away" had come from the other side, Alison hadn't let it stop her. She had opened the door, crossed to the bed where Heather was sprawled, and sat down.

For a moment Heather hadn't said anything, then lifting tear-stained eyes to Alison, she'd whispered, "I guess you're awfully mad at me, aren't you?"

Alison fought back the tears. "No, I'm not mad at you. Disappointed, but not mad."

Heather seemed to digest that for another long moment, then asked, "How soon do you plan to marry him...and move?"

"Not until you have a chance to get to know him," she said quietly. "Does that make you feel better?"

Heather nodded, but still refrained from looking at Alison. "I know I'm behaving like a bratty twelve-year-old, but for so long it's been just you and me...."

Alison hugged her tightly. "Don't worry, I'll never let anything or anyone come between us." She paused with a smile. "Suppose you repair your face and let's get June and hit the shopping mall."

Now, as Alison got out of her car, she couldn't say the shopping spree had been a success. While Heather had been polite, and at times her usual sweet self, there was a barrier between them, a barrier that Alison hadn't been able to dismantle.

Swallowing a sigh, she turned her gaze next door. Even before it registered that Rafe and Tom were standing in front of the portable building talking, she noticed that only a handful of trees remained. With Christmas still three weeks away, she was ecstatically surprised.

When she slammed the car door, both men looked her way. Tom smiled and waved. Rafe did neither. He merely walked toward her, but she could tell by the expression on his face that he was uptight, angry.

"Hi," was all she said, falling in step beside him instead of flinging her arms around him, as she longed to do.

For an instant, his stony gaze softened, but only for an instant. "I started working on the shop after lunch," he said, as if making polite conversation with a stranger. "Tom wanted to work the lot, so I let him."

Alison tried not to let his aloofness upset her, but she couldn't help it. He seemed hell-bent on shutting her out, and it hurt. Keeping her voice even was an effort. "I'm proud for you. It means your hard work with the trees has paid off."

"Yeah," he said in a clipped tone, at the same time pushing open the door and standing aside for her to enter.

The cozy warmth of the room acted as a soothing balm to her jagged nerves. But she didn't have a chance to head for the crackling fireplace. The second the door closed behind them, Rafe swung her around and took her into his arms with a swift urgency that almost frightened her.

"I wasn't sure you'd come," he whispered, a desperate note in his voice.

She pulled slightly away so that she could see his face. "How could you have doubted?"

"Oh, I doubted all right," he said tersely, "especially after the police showed up here and all but accused me of breaking and entering."

"Oh, Rafe, I'm so sorry. I know how painful it must have been."

"It made me madder than hell, that's what it did. The first crime that's committed in this town after I get back, and the local boys immediately tag me." His mouth was a thin, white line, indicating the depths of his rage.

"I'm sorry," she said again, trying to temper his anger.

"Me too, but unfortunately being sorry won't get them off my back. I'm sure there will be another one around soon, sniffing at my heels, watching every move I make."

"No, there won't."

Rafe hesitated, as if at first he didn't grasp her meaning. Then dropping his arms from around her, he asked warily, "How do you know?"

"Because the police also came to my house this morning."

"And?"

"And . . . and I told them the truth."

He grasped her arms again. "You mean you admitted you were with me last night?"

"All night," she whispered softly, staring up at him with her heart in her eyes.

His features contorted. "Oh, God, Alison, didn't you stop to think how damaging such a confession could be for you, what it will most certainly do to your reputation? And here you are about to go into business . . ."

Reaching out, Alison placed a finger against his lips, cutting him off. "I have no regrets," she said in a husky whisper. "No way was I going to let the law arrest an innocent man, especially not the man I'm going to marry."

He stared at her with a strange light in his eyes, while his mouth worked as if he was trying to find the right words but couldn't. With a muttered groan, he pulled her against him once more and buried his face in the side of her neck. "You're something else, you know that?"

Being in his arms, Alison told herself, was the only thing that mattered. It seemed unfair that so many obstacles should be in their path. It should be so simple—to go to him, to be a part of him. Only it wasn't.

She spoke her thoughts. "I wish things were easier for us, my darling. All I want is the freedom to love you," she said, moving out of his arms and walking to the fireplace where she bent and warmed her hands. "Happiness shouldn't be so hard to come by."

He came up behind her and dropped his hand on her shoulders. "What do you mean?"

"It's Heather," Alison said in a dull voice without turning around.

"I should have known."

"When I told the officer about us, she was in the room. So was June."

Rafe muttered a sharp expletive.

She faced him, her lips curved in a facsimile of a smile. "My thoughts exactly, only I didn't have the luxury of saying so."

"How did she take it?"

"Not so well. Since I couldn't soften the blow, it was a definite shock in more ways than one." Alison smiled without humor. "I had it planned in my mind how you two were going to meet and get to know one another. Afterward, I would tell her we were getting married." She shrugged. "Unfortunately that didn't pan out. Still, I wasn't prepared for her violent reaction."

Rafe ran his hands over his hair. "How old did you say she was?"

"Twenty."

"Isn't that a little old to be having temper tantrums?"

"Of course it is. But I can understand where she's coming from. Her security is threatened."

"Marrying me doesn't mean you're deserting her."

"She depends on me," Alison said carefully. "She knows she can come to me any time of the night or day. I'm her anchor. She counts on me not to change."

"Then it's time she learned better," he said. "Nothing ever stays the same, Alison. Everything changes. She'll have to get used to the idea. It'd just as soon be now."

A defensive feeling began to well up inside her, but she breathed deeply and thrust it aside. It was understandable, she told herself, that Rafe would be unsympathetic toward Heather. After all, he didn't know her.

"Of course, she'll learn better." Alison spoke with patience. "Naturally, the older she gets, the less she'll need me."

"How much older does she have to get before you cut the apron string?"

A shot of adrenaline-laced anger raced through Alison, and she froze for a split second, then recovered. "She isn't tied to my apron strings. Why, she has a boyfriend she's crazy about." She paused. "That's part of the problem."

A flicker of pain crossed Rafe's face, and instantly Alison wished she could retract her words.

"Heather's embarrassed, is that it?" he demanded, his voice tight with controlled bitterness. "Embarrassed that her sister's involved with an ex-con." Without looking at her, he sat down on her desk chair that he'd pulled close to the fire earlier and stared into the leaping flames.

There was a definite chill in the air outside, though inside it was toasty warm. Still Alison shivered, feeling the breech between her and Rafe widen once again.

Panicking, Alison closed the distance between them, and pushing his hands aside, sat on his lap. "Rafe, please try to understand. Just bear with me—and Heather," she pleaded, placing her hands on either side of his face. "I want you to meet her this week. After that, I'm certain things will begin to sort themselves out."

"Don't count on it being too easy, Alison. The valuable things in life don't come cheap. You have to pay for them."

She drew back. "What do you mean?"

"You know what I mean. Happiness doesn't come without its price, nor does anything else that's worth a damn. I've never known a scared person to be a happy one."

"And you think I'm scared?"

"Only you can answer that," he said soberly.

"Maybe I am. I don't know. But what I do know is that I can't bear the thought of you losing faith in me," she said, pressing against him as if she could soak up his strength and certainty.

"Then fight for us," he urged roughly.

She clung to him, felt the coarse fabric of his shirt scrape her cheek. "Rafe, hold me. Don't ever let me go."

"I have no intention of letting you go," he said thickly. "Ever."

He kissed her then, a deep, soul-searching kiss that ignited a response so deep inside her that she returned his kiss with a sudden, almost violent need.

"Oh, Alison," he groaned.

Suddenly kissing wasn't enough. She needed more, and he wanted more. His kisses became deeper, hotter, wetter.

She groaned as he dragged his mouth off hers and lifted her sweater so that he could get to the soft flesh underneath. Instantly, the straps of her teddy were stripped from her shoulders, spilling her full breasts into his hands.

"Oh, Rafe," she cried excitedly, as his moist lips locked on first one distended nipple, then the other.

Feeling the tug-of-war of his lips and tongue set her on fire. Whimpering, she shifted so that she had access to the zipper on his jeans. Moments later he was released into her hand.

He drew in a sharp, guttural breath. "Oh, Alison, oh, yes," he gasped, his eyes glazed. "I want you here. I want to be inside you. Right now."

"Yes, right now," she cried incoherently, encouraging him as he reached for the button on the waistband of her slacks. Nothing mattered except him becoming a part of her. Not the time, the place, or the circumstances.

With her help, he managed to rid her of all her clothes except the lacy teddy, which posed no problem. He simply popped the snaps between her thighs. Then lifting her slightly, he sat her down on his lap, but with her back to him.

Positioning his hands on her shoulders, he began kneading them slowly, gently, until her head lobbed forward, exposing her creamy neck. His lips replaced his hands, nipping tenderly on the sensitive area.

She could feel the enormous strength of his arms as he lifted her up and guided her down on him. She gasped as his hard strength penetrated her wet warmth, embedding himself high into her. She ached to move.

"Not yet," he whispered.

One hand moved across her stomach, fingers probing, seeking; the other concentrated on her breasts, her nipples, which soon began to throb along with her entire body.

It was a rare, lethal pleasure. Any second she expected to be consumed by the fire he was fanning inside her. Twisting around so that she was facing him, she sought his mouth, clung to him as together they rode the crest of a fulfillment that was more consuming, more frenzied than anything they had ever known.

Afterward her head fell onto his shoulder and he stopped moving.

"I love you," he whispered.

She sat still, sudden panic holding her motionless. Why was she here in the arms of this man whom she loved but did not really know? Why did love have to have such ragged, sharp edges?

She pulled back and looked at Rafe. He seemed so vulnerable. She felt she'd rather die than bring more hurt to him. "And I love you," she whispered.

Why, then, was she so afraid?

Sixteen

During the next few days Alison existed in a cocoon of happiness. Yet hovering on the outside was that fear of the unexpected, the unknown. She ignored it, unwilling to let anything disturb her euphoric state. When she was with Rafe, as she was almost every hour of every day, the flaw was easy to disregard. Today was no exception.

Once his Christmas trees were all sold, he had started in earnest remodeling her shop and completing the log cabin.

He had already made great strides in changing the appearance of the houses, especially the shop. It looked like she was definitely going to meet her self-imposed deadline.

Rafe assumed that once she caught up with her own work, which entailed unpacking freight filled with silk flowers, numerous containers and other items pertinent to her trade, she would be content and eager to remain with him while he worked. And this turned out to be true.

Dressed in baggy jeans, a red sweatshirt and Reeboks, she sat perched on the edge of her desk chair, watching as he sanded a shelf. Bending over the wood, his face was relaxed, completely caught up in what he was doing.

Alison found herself fascinated by the hand that held the sandpaper. It moved with loving tenderness across the wood, the way it had roamed her body, both last night and this morning, until she was like soft putty in his hands.

In the warmth of the house, Alison grew drowsy. She closed her eyes for a moment's rest.

Rafe chuckled. "Aha, caught you. Fine company you are."

"I wasn't asleep," she denied airily. "I was watching every move you made."

He laughed. "Yeah."

For the longest moment, she couldn't take her eyes off him. When he laughed, he looked so young, so carefree, so everything she wasn't. Sighing, Alison turned away.

"Something's bothering you, isn't it?" Rafe asked, his tone low and intense.

Knowing it was useless to try to fool him as he had an uncanny knack for reading her thoughts, she faced him again and smiled weakly. "I guess I'm just feeling sorry for myself."

"What about?" he asked, laying down the sandpaper and leaning against the wall. He propped himself up with a booted foot.

"Heather, I guess. She still refuses to accept that there is an 'us.'"

Her sister hadn't come home unannounced since she had learned about Rafe. When Alison had called and checked on her, Heather's excuses had ranged from studying for midsemester finals to rehearsing for the Christmas play. While those excuses were valid, Alison knew the real reason why Heather kept her distance. She was dodging a meeting with Rafe.

However, Alison wasn't going to let her get away with it.

Suddenly aware that Rafe had resumed his work, though without the enjoyment of a minute ago, she ended the silence.

"Heather's in a play tomorrow evening. What do you think about driving up, watching it, then taking her out to dinner?"

Rafe met her gaze. "That's fine by me. The sooner the better, especially since I want us to get married Christmas day."

Feeling her face drain of color, Alison stood abruptly. "I...I don't think that's possible. That'll barely give Heather time to..." The hard, closed look on his face stopped her.

"To what? To decide whether she approves or is willing? Or both?"

"Why the rush, Rafe?" she asked softly. "Anyway, you promised to give me time. I can't deliberately hurt her."

"But you'll let her hurt you?"

Alison balled a fist. "No, you're wrong. I'll make my own decision."

"We'll see," he muttered gruffly, reaching for her. "We'll see."

Alison couldn't stop her lips from trembling when they meshed with his.

In a cubbyhole that served as a dressing room backstage, Alison looked on while Heather slipped into a calf-length skirt and matching sweater. She had already removed her stage makeup and recombed her hair.

Heather's face, as she took great pains with the button at her waist, was so intensely solemn that Alison felt an impulse to giggle. That, she knew, would never do. Still, she wished she had some way of defusing the tension that was building in the small room.

"Rafe won't bite you, you know," Alison said, smiling in spite of herself.

Heather flashed her an exasperated look.

Suppressing a sigh, Alison said, "Come on, Rafe's waiting. Just be yourself, and you'll bowl him over."

"Sure, sis," Heather said drolly.

Rafe stood in the hallway outside the door. Swelling with pride at how handsome he was in slacks and a pullover sweater, Alison reached for his hand and smiled.

"Rafe, my sister, Heather."

Rafe disentangled his hand from Alison's and held it out to Heather. "Hello," he said in a pleasant tone.

"Hello," Heather answered sullenly, though she didn't reject his hand.

Alison watched the interplay carefully, but she couldn't tell whether the smile on Rafe's lips was amusement or a smirk. However, when he spoke again, his tone was as even and pleasant as before.

"You were sensational in the play. I enjoyed it very much."

His praise seemed to surprise Heather. Where before she had avoided looking directly at him, now she faced him squarely, showing a slight crack in her defenses. "You really think so?"

"Yeah, I really think so."

The animation in Heather's face suddenly disappeared. "How would you know anything about plays?" she asked rudely. "After all—"

"Heather!"

Ignoring Alison as if she hadn't spoken, Rafe drawled tolerantly, "You're right, I don't know much about them. I just know what I like, and I liked you a helluva lot in that one."

To Alison's relief, Heather had no comeback, obviously disconcerted by Rafe's disarming and unflappable show of confidence.

Heather refrained from speaking until they were in the car en route to the restaurant of her choosing. Then cutting her eyes at Rafe, she asked, "When are you planning to marry my sister?"

"If I had my way, it'd be tomorrow."

Heather fidgeted in the seat. "And live where?" she asked tersely.

"At the farm."

"You mean in that . . . that house?"

"How do you know what his house looks like?" Alison demanded with shocked fervor.

Heather eyed Alison defiantly. "I found out where he lived and drove there the other day. It . . . looks like it's falling down."

"It is," Rafe said before Alison had a chance to speak again. "But that's not the house we'll be living in." He flashed Heather an easy smile. "I think you'll be pleasantly surprised when you see the new one I've built."

Heather looked skeptical. "I didn't see any new house."

"That's because you didn't know where to look." Rafe glanced down at Alison. "You want to tell her?"

"Tell me what?"

He told her about the log house.

"That's nice," was Heather's only comment. It was all Alison could do not to grab her and shake her. Sitting close to Rafe was her salvation. She drew strength from his calm, a calm that she knew must be hard to maintain in light of Heather's hostility. She had never loved him more or been more afraid than in that moment.

Over dinner Alison realized that nothing short of a miracle could salvage the evening. Heather behaved incorrigibly, speaking only when spoken to, mumbling at that. Again the urge to shake her sister was so acute that Alison dug her nails into her palms. Making a desperate effort to make up for Heather's rudeness, she kept the conversation going between her and Rafe. He responded good-naturedly, overlooking Heather's petulant behavior.

Once the plates were removed and before coffee was served, Heather ended the ordeal. Looking at Alison, she said, "If you don't mind, I need to get back. I have a big test in the morning."

Later, curled up beside Rafe in his bed following a feverish session of lovemaking, Alison whispered, "I'm sorry."

He didn't pretend to misunderstand. "It could've been worse."

"No, I don't think so," she said, heartsick.

"We did our best."

"I know, but . . ."

"Shh, don't dwell on it. Right now I've got something else in mind," he said thickly. "Something much better."

"Oh, Rafe," she cried, holding him tighter, relishing the feel of him around her, inside her.

Alison struck out twice in a row. The dinner party she gave two days later fared no better than the evening with Heather.

Her aim in having it was to properly introduce Rafe to her closest friends, to show them that he was no longer the irresponsible boy who'd once got into trouble, but a strong, responsible man who was capable of making her happy.

The evening had started out well enough. She'd taken great pains with her Christmas decorations, and the house looked like something out of *House Beautiful*.

Rafe had done his part as well, despite the fact he hadn't been excited about the party. He'd gone along because he'd known how important it was to her. He had been easily the most attractive man there. The conservative blue suit and white shirt had been a startling contrast to both his tan and his blue eyes.

However, shortly after the guests had arrived and Rafe was introduced, a tension had filled the room, even though June had done her part to dispel it.

She had come up to Rafe, and following a swift but thorough perusal, stuck out a hand.

"I've looked forward to meeting you, Rafe Beaumont," she told him sincerely. "Any friend of Alison's is a friend of mine."

"Same here," Rafe said with courteous ease.

June's enthusiasm should have set the tone for the entire evening, but it hadn't. While the men seemed to accept Rafe readily enough, the women did not. Besides June, Myra, and Natalie and their husbands, there had been several other couples in attendance.

Throughout the evening Alison had circulated among the guests, pausing often to glance at Rafe, who would wink at her with quiet amusement. However, that hadn't been enough to keep her smile intact, especially after she'd overheard snatches of offensive conversation.

"Can you imagine? Why, he's the last person in the world I'd have expected her to marry...."

"...By looking at them together, you'd never realize she's that much older than he is...."

"... I wonder if he knows how lucky he is, getting a wife who's so wealthy...."

After hearing that last statement, Alison had fled into the kitchen, seething, her cheeks splotched with color. But there she'd found no relief.

Myra, dressed in the latest and gaudiest selection in her wardrobe, confronted her the second she entered the room.

"My, my, Alison dear, you've certainly stirred up a hornet's nest. Everybody, and I mean everybody is talking about you and Rafe."

Before Alison could get a word in edgewise, Myra went on, "I'll have to give you credit, darling, you certainly put one over on us. But how you lured a man like *him* to your bed is what I'm dying to hear."

By the time the last guest had departed, Alison had been shaking on the inside. To make matters worse, Rafe, instead of remaining behind and taking her into his arms, had followed the last guest to the door.

Gazing down at her, his relaxed, undisturbed state had no longer been in evidence. His features were unyielding.

"Was it as bad as I think it was?" she whispered.

"Worse, only because of how it affected you."

"I'm ... sorry."

"Me, too, only not for myself. Personally I could give a sweet damn what they think about me. But what does bother me is that you care what they think about you, about us."

"No, you're wrong," Alison stressed, feeling something akin to panic rise in her throat. "What they think about me, about us doesn't matter. I love you. Nothing can change that.''

''I hope not,'' he said flatly.

Without so much as a kiss on the cheek, he turned and walked to his car, leaving her standing in the doorway alone.

Early the following morning Alison walked through the large house, her thoughts in chaos. Was she unconsciously driving a wedge between her and Rafe?

So engrossed was she in trying to answer that question that she didn't hear the side door open. It wasn't until she heard movement behind her that she rallied and whirled around. Heather stood just inside the kitchen, sobs racking her body.

''Heather, my God!'' Alison cried. ''What happened?''

Seventeen

———

Heather, still sobbing, couldn't seem to get sufficient air into her lungs to reply. Holding her tightly, Alison waited. Something terrible had happened, but what? Alison forced a calm she was far from feeling.

"Please, tell me what this is all about."

Heather managed to stop crying long enough to whisper, "No. I just want to go to my room. I'll...I'll be all right."

"You're not going anywhere until you tell me what's going on," Alison said sternly, but gently, pulling out a chair at the table. "Here, sit down. I'll fix you a cup of tea."

Shortly, she sat the cup in front of Heather, who was busy mopping her tears with a Kleenex.

"This...this is something I have to work out on my own," Heather said huskily.

Alison sat down. "Does it have something to do with Tim?"

A new onslaught of tears fell heavily down Heather's cheeks. "Yes." The word was barely audible.

"Did you break up?" Alison pressed cautiously.

"Yes...no." Heather shook her head. "I don't know. We...we had a terrible fight."

Alison sighed. "Why can't you tell me about it? We've always shared everything?"

Heather's face was a study in misery. "Don't you understand, sis? I can't tell you!"

Alison sat still. "It was about me, wasn't it?" she asked, amazed that her voice was steady. "That's why you won't tell me."

The flush on Heather's face deepened.

"What happened? I want to know."

Heather pushed damp strands of hair away from her face. "We...we were arguing about nothing really, just something silly. Then all at once Tim...Tim lashed out about you and Rafe, said everyone in town was talking about you marrying an ex-con."

Blind rage overcame Alison at the unjustness of it all. "And what does he think about it? Tim, I mean."

"He...he said it didn't matter to him, but I know better," Heather wailed. "He minds. That's why we fought."

"I'm sorry you were humiliated on my account," Alison said, her stomach twisting as she envisioned the scene.

"Oh, Alison, I hate myself for acting like such a ninny, but—I've been so miserable. Everything seems to be falling apart, and I can't stop it."

"Does it upset you that much that I'm going to marry Rafe?"

"I don't know," Heather said. "I guess I'm all mixed up. It just seems—oh, I don't know how to say it. It's just that we've been so happy here. I didn't realize how much it all meant—home and you and being together. I was such a fool. I thought it could go on forever."

"The only thing that won't ever change, my darling, is my love for you," Alison said, reaching over and touching Heather's flushed cheek. "As long as you remember that, you have nothing to fear."

"Oh, sis, I love you, really I do, and I'm sorry if I hurt you, only..." Heather's voice broke again.

"Shh, no more tears. I promise everything's going to be all right."

An hour later Heather left to go back to the university. The instant the door closed behind her, Alison made her way to the couch and sank wearily onto it. The scene with Heather had left her feeling limp, as if the bones had been drawn from her body.

She'd known that loving Rafe would carry a high price tag, only she hadn't guessed how high. And while she could never give him up, she couldn't marry him right now either. She simply needed more time. Even if he proved reluctant to accept the further delay, she knew in the end she could convince him because he loved her and she loved him.

After all, who could argue with love?

* * *

"Good morning."

"Good morning," Alison whispered, clutching the phone. "I was just thinking about you."

"I hope it was good, especially after the way I acted last night."

"Well, we were both a little uptight."

"I know how to take care of that," Rafe said huskily.

"Me, too."

He cleared his throat. "I have a surprise for you."

"You finished with the shop?"

"Yep."

"Oh, Rafe, that's wonderful."

His tone changed. "When am I going to see you?"

"In a while. We have to talk."

"What's wrong?" His words cut like a whiplash through the wires.

"Heather."

He sighed. "What's happened now?"

"She came home from SFA a little while ago in a state."

"Is she all right?"

"For now," Alison said dully.

"What does that mean?"

"I'll explain when I see you."

Rafe didn't answer for a moment, and when he did, his voice was flat, controlled. "I'll be at the shop."

"Okay, I'll . . . see you later."

"Alison."

"Yes."

"I love you."

Alison squeezed back the tears. "I love you, too."

* * *

No matter how hard he tried, Rafe couldn't shake the premonition of disaster that seemed to have him by the throat. Until Alison got there and he took her into his arms, he didn't see any way to shake that feeling and put things back in perspective.

He wished she were there with him now. No, better yet, he wished they were at the farm and she was in bed beside him, holding him. He loved her body, her long, pale legs and her lovely full breasts. But more than that, he loved her—loved her mind, her laughter, her kindness, her gentleness.

"You heal me, Alison," he'd told her once, and he'd meant it. That was why he was so scared, scared he was losing her.

Pausing in his thoughts, he listened, thinking he'd heard the front door open.

"Alison, is that you?"

"Sorry, old boy, you're stuck with me," Tom said, striding into the room.

Rafe hid his disappointment behind a smile. "What the hell brings you around here this time of day?"

"Gayle told me to get lost. She wanted to clean the house."

Rafe laughed. "Well, now that you're here, what do you think?"

Tom's eyes circled what used to be the living room of the old house. "I think you've done a damn good job."

"Kinda thought so myself."

Tom grinned. "But it's what Alison thinks that counts."

"She's pleased."

"By the way, how's your house coming? Finished with it yet?"

"All but a little trim here and there. Now, it's up to Alison."

Tom angled his head. "So I guess you two will be tying the knot soon, huh?"

"I don't know." Rafe snarled the answer.

"Did I say something wrong?"

The pain was bad, but he forced the words out. "I'm losing her, Tom."

"Losing her?" A sigh came from Tom's big chest. "What makes you say a crazy thing like that?"

"Gut instinct, that's what," Rafe said, his brows beetled with intensity as he eyed his friend.

"Gut instinct ain't always reliable," Tom drawled, though his features registered concern.

"In this case it is."

"What's the problem?"

"Her sister for one. She's pitching a fit."

"If you ask me, she needs her butt spanked."

"Too late for that." Rafe's tone was dry.

"What else?"

"It's Alison herself," Rafe said, feeling suddenly hollow inside. "Maybe she's getting cold feet about marrying an ex-con."

Clearly aggravated, Tom leaned forward. "That's the craziest thing I've ever heard."

"Is it?"

"She loves you, dammit. It's written all over her. And anyway, she doesn't have a malicious bone in her body."

"You're right, but she keeps hedging. That's what scares me. She's the best thing that's ever happened to me, and I want to marry her so badly I can't stand it."

"Well, you know Gayle and I are pulling for you. And if there's anything we can do..."

Rafe swatted the air with his right hand. "I know, and thanks."

A short time later, when he was alone again, Rafe walked to the mantel. Instead of keeping his mind on what he was doing, he turned his thoughts back to Alison.

"Face it, Beaumont," he whispered aloud. "She's going to break your damn heart."

When Alison let herself in the door of Silk Reflections, Rafe was standing by the fireplace, working. He looked so big, so strong, so dear that tears sprang into her eyes.

Wordlessly, he laid down his tool and came toward her. With a muted cry she walked into his arms. For a long moment they were content to hold onto each other. Then Rafe tilted her chin back and kissed her, gently at first, then hungrily, greedily. Her lips clinging to his seemed to inflame him.

"Marry me, Alison, now. Today," he muttered wildly against her lips. "Don't make me wait any longer."

Gasping for both air and strength, Alison gently maneuvered out of his arms, though her gaze never wavered. "Oh, Rafe," she wailed. "I—"

"Please, Alison, no more excuses. I don't want to hear them."

"Oh, Rafe, please, it's not that simple. Just listen to me. It's not that I don't want to marry you now, it's that I can't."

"Can't or won't? There's a difference." The anger in his voice was like a sharp wedge.

"I know there's a difference," she said, nervously licking her lips. "That's why we have to talk."

"I'm listening."

"You know I told you Heather came home earlier. Well, she'd had a fight with her boyfriend about... about us."

"Go on."

Alison repeated almost word for word what Heather had told her. When Rafe didn't respond, she went on, a pleading note in her voice, "So you can surely see now why we can't rush into anything. She... has to have more time to adjust."

"You just don't see it, do you?"

Alison blinked hard. "See what?"

"See that she's using you, using your love to get her own way."

"No, you're wrong," Alison said, an ache beginning behind her eyes. "She's just confused about being uprooted, leaving the home where she feels secure."

"Oh, Alison, if it weren't that, it'd be something else. Believe me, in time she'll adjust."

"I'm not so sure," Alison said, unable to block out Heather's grief-stricken face.

"Well, if you're waiting to please your sister and your friends, you're fighting a losing battle because you never will.'' His words bit her. ''At some point you have to please yourself.''

Alison let her tone match his. ''I told you it's just not that simple.''

''Have you ever asked yourself why not?''

She hesitated. ''I don't understand what you mean.''

''Oh, I think you do. Are you sure it's Heather that's having trouble adjusting, or is it you?'' His features were haggard, drawn.

Suddenly Alison's anger faded, and a dull, dizzying sickness took its place. Was Rafe right? Was she harboring doubts that she didn't want to recognize? Was she indeed frightened of leaving everything near and dear to her and starting a life with someone whose life was so different from hers? No, of course she wasn't. She loved Rafe.

''That's ridiculous!'' she snapped.

''No, I'm sorry to say, it's not.''

''Oh, Rafe,'' Alison whispered brokenly, ''you're wrong. I love you desperately and I do want to share your life, but not at the expense of Heather. And since I can't come to you right now, I'm asking you to be patient, to understand.''

''How much longer, Alison?''

''I...don't know.''

''I see.''

Looking at him, she saw that his mouth was set stubbornly, even cruelly.

''What do you want, Rafe? Do you want me to beg you to see things my way, to give me the time I've asked for?''

"You know better than that!"

"I would if it'd prove to you how much I love you."

"Actions speak louder than words, Alison."

"Are you saying then that it has to be on your terms or not at all?"

"Don't make me the heavy in this, Alison. I'm not the one with the doubts, the insecurities." He paused, his lips set in a taut line. "I'm not the one who's the coward."

"That's not fair!" Alison cried. Then, trembling inside, she added more quietly, "I've made my decision. I won't be pushed into doing something I can't live with."

Suddenly the air felt very heavy, heavy with fear.

"It's over, is that what you're saying?"

"I'm sorry," Alison whispered, her body already feeling drained and empty.

"So am I," Rafe said so steadily she knew it was final.

Still she could not believe it when he simply turned and walked out the door, leaving her staring after him in a shocked and stricken astonishment.

For a second she stood as if paralyzed. He couldn't be gone. He just couldn't walk out and leave her like this, not if he loved her. A scream was collecting strength in her lungs. But she couldn't utter a sound.

Her knees wanted to give way; her body seemed to want to crumble into fragments as a strangling disappointment and rebellion possessed her.

Rafe! she wept in silent agony.

Eighteen

During the next few weeks, pain followed Alison around like a silent shadow. Christmas came and went; she hardly noticed. She had opened Silk Reflections, but the thrill was gone.

Nothing had changed. The empty evenings and barren weekends looked as they had before, adding additional weight to Alison's drooping spirits.

Yet everything had changed. Inside herself, she was different; she had loved a second time, so deeply and completely that she was an entirely different person.

Only around her customers and Heather did she make an effort to dig herself out of her depressed state. To Heather she had stated briefly that she no longer intended to marry Rafe, that things had not worked out. At times, though, she suspected Heather knew something was amiss because during the holidays she went out of her way to be attentive. As for her friends, June was the only one she had confided in, and even then she hadn't gone into detail.

While Alison despised herself for not having the strength to shake the pain inside her, she couldn't seem to help it, despite the fact that good things were happening around her. Heather and Tim had patched things up between them; Tim had apologized to both her and Heather. The couple was now engaged, and Alison couldn't have been more pleased. Her friends had accepted her back into the fold, having assured her that she'd made the right decision by not marrying Rafe.

But most of all, her goal had been realized; her store was a huge success. She had held fast to her dream and had made it work. However, it was a bittersweet victory. Without Rafe to share in her good fortune, it was meaningless.

She constantly ached for Rafe, walked around with a hole inside her, as if part of her was missing.

Returning home from the shop late one evening brought no relief. The moment she opened the door, loneliness sank its tentacles into her. Yet she wasn't sorry about Rafe. Their brief affair had been the best time of her life.

Dropping her paraphernalia down in a chair in the den, Alison walked toward the kitchen and glanced out the window. The weather was worsening by the second; it had begun to rain. The winter evening matched her mood, she thought bleakly.

"Hi, sis."

A hand flew to her throat, and for a minute Alison couldn't move. Then spinning around, she glared at Heather. "You nearly scared me out of ten years' growth."

"Sorry," Heather responded quickly. "Didn't mean to. Just wanted to surprise you."

Now that her heart was beating at a normal rate again, Alison smiled. "You did that, all right. I had no idea you were home. Where's you car?"

"Tim dropped me off, and as soon as he left, I lay down and went sound asleep. Didn't wake up until I heard the front door slam."

"Well, I'm glad to see you. Are you going to spend the night?"

"Yep."

"Good," Alison said, relieved that the evening wouldn't be the disaster she'd anticipated. "As soon as I change clothes, I'll fix us a bite to eat. In the meantime, why don't you get the fire started?"

Later, sitting on opposite ends of the couch, drinking coffee, Heather stared at Alison with a troubled look on her face.

"The shop's still doing well, isn't it?"

Alison smoothed out a pleat on her pants. "Oh, yes, far beyond my expectations."

"Then why are you so unhappy?"

Alison was startled. The Heather of old would never have been this astute. Love had definitely matured her sister. While Alison was glad to see it, it had come too late for her.

"Well, we all have our days when we're in the doldrums," Alison began evasively, still reluctant to discuss Rafe with anyone. It was much too painful.

"That's not what I meant, and you know it."

Alison didn't say anything.

"You've lost weight and if you smile—not when, mind you—it's like it's being pulled out of you."

"You're imagining things," Alison said more sharply than she intended.

"Am I?" Heather shook her head. "I don't think so. It's Rafe, isn't it?"

"Heather—"

"You never told me why you called off the wedding."

Alison felt the color rise to her cheeks. "It...it just didn't work out, that's all," she said carefully.

"Because of me." Heather's voice wavered slightly. "I was the reason it didn't work out, wasn't I?"

"Heather, please, I don't want to discuss it, if you don't mind." Alison looked away and raised a hand to her forehead. "There were lots of reasons."

"Is...it too late? I mean is it possible—"

Alison interrupted. "No, it's not possible."

"Will you forgive me for acting like a selfish jerk?"

"Oh, Heather, honey, you're not to blame, at least not entirely. It's much more complicated than that. If you don't mind, let's drop the subject. Anyway, you need to finish your coffee so we can get to bed. I'm beat."

Thirty minutes later Alison walked into her silent and dark bedroom. Quickly undressing, she showered, then climbed into bed, fighting down the shakiness that assailed her. Nights were her worst times.

Even though Rafe had never shared this bed with her, it was him she thought about, him she longed for each time she crawled in between the cold sheets. Cuddling into a fetal position, she let the tears have free rein. Rafe hadn't loved her, not like she'd loved him, or he wouldn't have walked out. She was going to have to come to terms with that as well as learning to live alone again.

One more time.

Alison took pains with her dressing the following morning. She had scheduled her first sale in her shop for today, and she hoped it would be packed. As a result, she wanted to look her best. But there was an ulterior motive as well. By exaggerating her dress, she hoped to buoy her drooping spirits.

She chose a two-piece, salmon-colored suit, black heels and gold earrings. Then she draped a brightly colored scarf around her neck.

Confident that if nothing else she looked her best, Alison waved at Heather and Tim, who were backing out the drive in front of her. As soon as they were out of sight, she got into her own car.

She was concentrating so hard on her driving, as the roads were slick from last night's rain, that she almost missed the truck that pulled out of the intersection a few yards in front of her.

Alison's heart lurched and faltered. Her hands turned icy around the steering wheel.

"Rafe," she whispered aloud, keeping a frantic eye on him, afraid he was a figment of her imagination. She watched as he guided the truck in and out of traffic.

Even before she recognized the vehicle, she had known it was him. His hair was longer, and his arm, extended out the window, seemed more muscular than she remembered, but it was Rafe. Oh, God, it was Rafe.

Tears blurred her vision while her heart hammered out of control. "Why now?" she whispered aloud, feeling as if someone or something heavy were standing on her chest, crushing it.

Then just as quickly as he'd appeared, he disappeared, leaving a pain of despair inside her so deep, so cutting that for a moment she thought she might die.

That was when she heard the horn. Blinking, Alison jerked her head around and watched in horror as a car skidded toward her. She opened her mouth, but nothing came out. Quickly, violently, she gripped the wheel and twisted it.

Her actions were too little too late. When the impact came, Alison's head fell forward and she knew no more.

"Alison, can you hear me?"

"Yes," she whispered between parched lips. "Where...where am I?"

"In the emergency room at the hospital," the same kind voice responded, a voice that she finally recognized.

Quickly opening her eyes, Alison stared up into the face that belonged to the voice. "Dr. Boyd . . . is that you?"

"Yes, my dear, it's me."

"What . . . happened? Why am I here?"

The doctor frowned. "You don't remember?"

Alison shut her eyes, and when she did, the horror came rushing back to her. "Oh, no," she cried, feeling the tears burn the back of her eyelids. "The people in the other car, are they—"

"Shh," Dr. Boyd soothed. "The only occupant of the other car was a Mr. Blanton, and he wasn't hurt, not even a scratch. You were damned lucky yourself that you came out of this with only a slight concussion."

Alison struggled to sit up. Once her legs were dangling off the side of the bed, she looked around. She and the doctor were alone in the small, clinically clean room. He was scrutinizing her from under a shelf of bushy white eyebrows.

"Thank God no one else paid for my foolishness," Alison said, straightening her clothes.

Dr. Boyd leaned against the cabinet and folded his arms across his chest. "What happened? Did you black out or something?"

"No, I didn't, though I will admit something happened to upset me, and I wasn't paying attention to what I was doing."

"Looks like a lot's been happening to upset you lately."

Alison looked away, unable to meet his probing eyes. Since she came to Monroe, Doctor Boyd had been her doctor. While at times his bedside manner was abrupt, it didn't matter because he was a crackerjack physician. She had confidence in him and recognized that under that briskness was a caring man. When Carter had died, he had helped her immensely.

"I don't know what you mean?" Alison said at last.

"Oh, I think you do. A person doesn't lose ten pounds or better over a relatively short period of time and something not be wrong, unless they're on a diet, of course. And we both know that's not the case with you, right?"

"Right."

"Want to tell me what's bothering you, then?"

Alison shook her head, unable to speak. The lump in her throat felt twice the size of the one on her head and hurt worse. Tears ran down her cheeks.

Dr. Boyd sighed. "I won't press you to confide in me, but I'm here if you need me." He paused and handed her a tissue out of the box behind him. "You're one lucky lady who should have been in the morgue instead of here in the emergency room. If you hadn't swerved that wheel when you did, causing him to hit you in the rear door, you'd definitely have been a statistic."

Alison reached up, and without taking her eyes off the doctor, felt the goose egg above her right eye. Flinching, she asked, "What are you saying?"

"I'm saying that the Man upstairs has obviously given you another chance. If I were you, I'd fix whatever had me all cut up inside, or learn to live with it, then get on with my life. Remember, most people don't get second chances, so don't squander yours."

Alison sat for a moment in a dazed stupor, the doctor's words beating inside her head like an offensive drum, repeating themselves over and over. Was he right? Was she squandering her life? Of course she was. The answer was just that simple and just that clear.

Her sister and her friends had controlled her life, directed it—but only because she had let them. She and she alone had denied life to herself. Again it was all so clear, so amazingly clear.

She was lonely because she chose to be. She was unfulfilled because she chose to be. She was existing in a misery of her own making because she chose to be.

Rafe was right. She had been such a coward, such a foolish coward, afraid to take a chance and run with it.

"Dr. Boyd, am I free to go?" she asked breathlessly.

An eyebrow quirked. "Yes, but only if you promise to get plenty of rest and come see me in a couple of days."

Once she was steady on her feet, Alison smiled through her tears and kissed him on his ruddy cheek. "Thanks so much. You'll never know how much you helped me."

She pulled off on the side of the road just before she turned into the drive that led to the farmhouse, wondering if Rafe had moved into the log house. The answer came easily. From where she sat, she could see the fire curling out of the chimney. Rafe hadn't gone anywhere.

Once she had spoken with the investigating officer who had been waiting outside the emergency room, one of Dr. Boyd's assistants had driven her home. Instead of going inside, however, she had gotten into Carter's Honda, which she hadn't sold, repaired her face as best she could with the makeup in her purse, and backed out of the drive, conscious that every nerve in her body was jumping.

There had been no time to think. There had been no decision to make.

Now, as she headed the car up the road, she tried to ward off a burgeoning fear. What if she had waited too long? What if he no longer wanted her?

By the time she got out of the car, that fear was a tangible constriction around her heart, a knot in her belly.

Five steps to the door.

Her heart slammed into her throat. She knocked and waited, her breathing ragged.

"It's open," Rafe muttered with shocking clarity.

Somehow Alison managed to come up with the strength to turn the knob. When she finally crossed the threshold, she saw the stove and the fire. And then Rafe.

He had been in the process of replenishing the stove, and was still bent over. When he saw her, he straightened to his full height and stared at her.

"Hello, Rafe," she whispered.

Her eyes blurred by tears, she took a tentative step toward him. His features wavered. She did not know if he was horrified or pleased, and she didn't care. She was too busy feasting on his lean, endearing figure through a swimming haze of firelight and shadow.

"Alison." He spoke her name, nothing more, though it sounded as if it had been dug out of him.

She felt a pull somewhere in the region of her chest. Was it scar tissue ripping away? Still she couldn't find the words to say what she'd come to say. Instead she stood before him, feeling an enormous humbleness.

"Rafe, can you forgive me?" she asked. Her voice was scratchy, unlike her own. She couldn't bring herself to look in his eyes. "I ... I'm sorry," she added brokenly.

It was impossible for her to say more. Her throat simply closed up. When she didn't think she could stand the silence another second, Rafe came toward her.

"Is it really you, Alison?" he asked with disbelief.

"Yes," she managed to eke out; her tongue felt weighted with lead.

"My God, what happened?" He spoke in a hoarse kind of whisper.

She lifted an unsteady hand to the knot on her head and tried to smile, even though her heart was breaking. "Let's just say I got a lick on the head that brought me to my senses, made me realize what I'd done ... to you ... to me."

"Alison," he said again, and by his voice, frayed and unfamiliar, she knew that he, too, was uncertain. "There are two kinds of people in this world, those who run and those who stay. God help me, but I'm one who stays." He took a step closer, leaving only a hairsbreadth between them. "I tried to stop loving you, I really did. But it didn't work."

"Oh, Rafe," she cried, lunging into his out-stretched arms, feeling the tears on his cheeks mingle with hers. "I love you and I never stopped. And if you still want me, I'll marry you tomorrow."

"If I still want you ..." Rafe broke off, struggling for breath.

She reached up and traced the deep grooves around his mouth. He trapped the finger between his lips and began sucking on it.

"Hold me," she groaned, feeling him tremble against her as he lowered his lips to hers.

They exchanged long, drugging kisses until they were both so weak they couldn't stand. Still trem-bling, Rafe swept her into his arms and carried her into the bedroom.

This time when they made love, they came together perfectly. They stroked each other tenderly, sweetly, then savagely, wildly. When he entered her, Alison whispered his name just as the storm raging inside them unleashed its fury.

"Oh, Rafe, don't ever let me go," she cried later, nestled against his heart. "Don't ever let me go."

"Never, my darling. I'll never let you go again."

And he didn't.

*   *   *   *   *

**A compelling novel of deadly revenge and passion
from bestselling international
romance author Penny Jordan**

POWER PLAY

Eleven years had passed but the
terror of that night was something
Pepper Minesse would never
forget. Fueled by revenge against
the four men who had brutally
shattered her past, she set in
motion a deadly plan to destroy
their futures.

Available in February!

SILHOUETTE DESIRE™

presents

AUNT EUGENIA'S TREASURES
by CELESTE HAMILTON

Liz, Cassandra and Maggie are the honored recipients of Aunt Eugenia's heirloom jewels...but Eugenia knows the real prizes are the young women themselves. Read about Aunt Eugenia's quest to find them everlasting love. Each book shines on its own, but together, they're priceless!

Available in December:
THE DIAMOND'S SPARKLE (SD #537)

Altruistic Liz Patterson wants nothing to do with Nathan Hollister, but as the fast-lane PR man tells Liz, love is something he's willing to take *very* slowly.

Available in February:
RUBY FIRE (SD #549)

Impulsive Cassandra Martin returns from her travels... ready to rekindle the flame with the man she never forgot, Daniel O'Grady.

Available in April:
THE HIDDEN PEARL (SD #561)

Cautious Maggie O'Grady comes out of her shell...and glows in the precious warmth of love when brazen Jonah Pendleton moves in next door.

SD-AET-1R

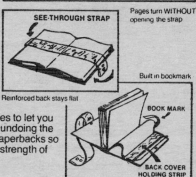

At long last, the books you've been waiting for
by one of America's top romance authors!

DIANA PALMER

DUETS

Ten years ago Diana Palmer published her very first
romances. Powerful and dramatic, these gripping tales
of love are everything you have come to expect from
Diana Palmer.

In March, some of these titles will be available again in
DIANA PALMER DUETS—a special three-book collec-
tion. Each book will have two wonderful stories plus an
introduction by the author. You won't want to miss them!

Book 1
SWEET ENEMY
LOVE ON TRIAL

Book 2
STORM OVER THE LAKE
TO LOVE AND CHERISH

Book 3
IF WINTER COMES
NOW AND FOREVER

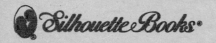 *Silhouette Books*®

DP-1

Silhouette Intimate Moments®

Available now ... it's time for

TIMES CHANGE
Nora Roberts

Jacob Hornblower is determined to stop his brother, Caleb, from making the mistake of his life—but his timing's off, and he encounters Sunny Stone instead. Their passion is timeless—but will this mismatched couple learn to share their tomorrows?

Don't miss Silhouette Intimate Moments #317

Get your copy now—while there's still time!
